To Zoe

Love

X gran Hart X

CW00857985

Northwind

"The author paints a wonderful picture with words, quickly transporting you into the heart of the story. What a perilous place the big wide world is for a little hedgehog, especially such an unusual one! The reader will quickly become attached to Northwind and the charming characters he encounters. A really touching book that will hopefully make people think about hedgehogs and how easy it is for us to help them."

Fay Vass, Chief Executive,

BRITISH HEDGEHOG PRESERVATION SOCIETY

*   *   *

"Northwind is a book that cherishes the long tradition of animal storytelling... The world moves on, but the truths of difference, danger, fear and friendship shine as bright as ever."

Ann Drysdale,

AUTHOR AND BROADCASTER

*   *   *

"What an enchanting story and the illustrations are gorgeous"

Sandi Thom,
Singer/songwriter/Producer
CEO Guardian Angels Music LLC

*   *   *

Northwind

Bob Rogers

Illustrated by
Rebecca Paul

For Elliott – 'Every life matters' – **B. R.**
For Jessie & Harri – 'Love you' – **R. P.**

First published in the UK in 2018 by Humble Bumble Books
Registered Office: Ragamuffins Emporium , Comercial Street, Pontypool, NP4 6XX

Text copyright © Bob Rogers 2018
Illustrations © Rebecca Paul 2018

The moral rights of Bob Rogers and Rebecca Paul to be identified as the author and illustrator of this work respectively have been asserted.

All papers used in the making of this book have been produced in accordance with systems free from elemental chlorine and are dedicated to responsible and sustainable forest management.

Printed and bound in the UK
ISBN 978-0-9565840-3-8
A CIP catalogue record for this book is available from the British Library.

www.humblebumblebooks.com

CONTENTS

IMAGINE

I magine it's the kind of day for paddling pools, sun hats and sloppy lotion; one of those days full of buzzing things and the smell of cut grass - a day when the most welcome sound of all is the jingling of the ice-cream van.

Imagine a day like that on a country lane far from town; on each side is a tangle of tall wildflowers and all sorts of colourful weeds.

Walking down the lane we come to an old gate that doesn't seem to have been opened for a very long time. It is tied by wire and faded rope to a pair of crumbling wooden posts. Looking over this gate we see a sloping field of wheat and beyond it a small wood. On a far corner is a little hill.

Now - enough of seeing; it's time to hear.

Lean on the gate and close your eyes (you can climb up and sit on it if you like, but be careful, it's a bit rickety).

Listen. You may hear very little at first, but if you are patient you will 'tune in' and all the sounds of the Great Outside will come to you.

The first things you hear may be the cries of birds, the chatter and buzz of insects or, if you are lucky, the barking of a distant fox. Of course, you may hear more familiar animals too; cattle, sheep, chickens or even the deep bass baying of the Basset who lives in the cottage at the bottom of the hill.

But if you come to this spot after dark you will hear a whole new chorus because night in the countryside is not quiet.

Owls call to each other beneath the stars, shy badgers cough or cry out in the deep black woods and somewhere from under the line of old hawthorn and hazel trees that separate the field from the lane come the grunts and snuffles of a patrolling hedgehog.

We might imagine all these noises are meaningless, but they are not. They are voices, just like yours and mine. After all, these creatures need to talk to each other.

We know that some animals understand a bit of human language and that some birds can even copy the people-noises they hear; so maybe, just maybe, all the barks and squeaks and clucks and snorts and grunts and whistles and scents and dances are a language the creatures use to tell their stories?

Because, you see, every one of them has a story to tell...

*   *   *

1

First You Need To Know

My name is…

…no, wait, that's not the first thing you need to know. The first thing you need to know is about being born; which happened to me, and you, and your parents, and the old dog you often see taking its human for a walk, and the fly buzzing against the window trying to get back to the Great Outside.

Being born is something we've all done - but few of us can remember it happening...

I was born on a wet and windy night at the time in the seasons when winter has gone but summer has not yet come to take its place. A fierce gale howled through the branches far above and big raindrops battered the leaves and grass beyond the entrance to my home.

Of course, I didn't see or hear any of this; having arrived, like all hedgehogs, with no sight or hearing. But before many hours had passed there came the scent of the rich damp earth and the comforting scuttling of my mother and my three fellow new-born hoglets close by. Two of these were my brothers and the third was my clever sister.

My first spines began to appear after just an hour, they were white and soft - just as all new born hoglets' spines are, but all we cared about then was the warmth of our home, Mother's milk and sleep. It's hard work being born, whatever kind of creature you are, and we were very tired.

During that very early time we drank milk and slept and woke and stretched our legs and scratched and yawned and then did it all over again. Sometimes Mother was there and sometimes we hoglets were left on our own. But we weren't afraid. What was there to fear? As far as we knew the whole of our existence was a little hollow of warm leaves and moss and 'Outside' was somewhere Mother went - nothing to do with us. We were content, unaware of the passing of days and nights in our little nest.

Then two awesome things took place almost one after the other. The first came during a change of position to try to get comfortable in a corner of the nest - which was a struggle as one of my siblings was also trying to occupy the same spot. Mother was out hunting.

Pushing into a soft pile of leaves caused... a noise! Whatever could that be? Stop; and the noise stopped; resume nosing about and... There it was again! Having never 'heard' anything before;

it took a little while to realise that it was my movements and actions which were responsible for it happening.

Then there were other noises, more rustling of leaves and... grunting. A small grunt echoed inside my head feeling so loud I squeaked in fright - which seemed even louder. Other grunts were coming from my siblings. How could this be? The little nest was suddenly alive with... 'sound.'

I could hear!

As soon as we realised the noises were harmless we couldn't stop ourselves. We grunted and squealed just for the sake of it, just to hear.

The noises became a chorus. We were all laughing now with the joy of experiencing sound. But, in a lull in our noise, there came something else - sounds from... the unknown place beyond our home.

There was the vast and scary rushing of the wind blowing across the field and through the branches of great trees in the nearby woods - although at that moment we had no idea what these things were. It was a deep and huge sound that seemed to fill the whole of... whatever was out there.

And there were other sounds. High-pitched calls and shouts and yells that moved quickly from place to place; these, we decided, could only be creatures like us, capable of moving around - but much faster.

What could they be? The noises seemed to be coming from far above. It was clear we were all as puzzled as each other.

Learning to communicate and share information is something all creatures need to do, but when you are small and vulnerable like we are, you must know how to do these things as soon as you are able.

It's not so much learning to speak as learning to understand; and it's not about a language but more of a sense of knowing what every other creature is trying to share with you. It just seems to happen; the snuffles and grunts and squeaks and snorts and barks and whistles of all creatures have meanings, and just as we know how to feed as soon as we are born we also somehow know what all the noises mean.

Not just noises, but movements and scents too. It's important, we need to warn each other of danger or share all kinds of information and all creatures understand this.

All creatures that is except birds - whose way of communicating is like ours but contains many sounds for things we can never experience - and the creatures who at that point none of us were aware of - known as humans, who use really odd sounds that no one but themselves can make sense of.

And so, in those first moments of hearing, we shared our curiosity.

'What do you think those noises are?'

'Things like us?'

'They're not speaking like us, are they?'

'They seem to come and go in that rushing sound.'

'Perhaps there are places where there is no ground and there are creatures that can live in a place like that?' (This from my brother, we all laughed.)

'How could something live without touching the ground?' scoffed my other brother.

As he was speaking, the second amazing thing began to happen...

It was just a faint kind of... non-dark at first...

'Is anyone else getting a funny... bright thing in their minds?' I asked. My two brothers still hadn't got over the surprise of being able to hear and were grunting and laughing at each other, but my sister responded.

'I've had that since... well since it was light then went dark and then became light again – there's a brightness which comes from the place that Mother uses to appear and disappear. Everything is getting clearer and clearer. I can see you, I can see you all.'

'You can... see me? What do you mean?'

A new 'time of light' was beginning beyond our home and it was flooding in.

My two brothers stopped their giggling and grunting as a sense of curiosity overtook us.

'I don't know how to put it,' my sister continued, 'I can... "see" you. I know what you look like, I know what is you and what is *not* you.' Even then, so soon after being born, my sister was the clever one and always first with new discoveries.

Neither of my brothers could see at this point and my vision was nothing more than the ability to detect the difference between light and dark.

'So, what do we look like then?' My question probably didn't make much sense to her, but we were discovering amazing new things and just didn't have anything to compare our experiences to.

'Well...,' she began, clearly struggling, 'from what I can make out, and judging by my own experiences, all the things we use to scent things and hear things and see things are on one end of a... thing, and the rest is covered in our prickly things and there are a number of things that are not sharp underneath us that we are using to move around on...'

My brothers began to laugh, 'Never heard anything like it!' The one said.

'Never heard anything at all until just now!' The other responded and they both fell about laughing again.

'It's what we look like anyway - and we all look the same, except for...'

'Except for what?' I asked

'Well,' she responded curiously.

'Except for you.'

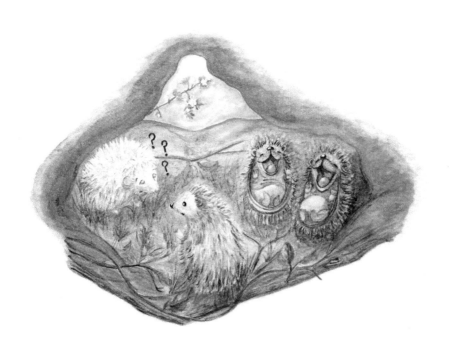

* * *

2

Everything Must Have a Name

'So what's different about me?'

My sister struggled to put words to what she saw;
'Well, you're the same shape and everything and all your bits seem
to be in the right places, it's just that you're... well, the light you
give off is... you're much, much lighter than the rest of us.'

'Lighter?'

'Lighter... brighter... I don't know how else to put it - and
your... *things-you-see-with* are different too - a very different kind of
light. In fact, I've never seen anything else that seems to be that
kind of light.'

The truth is, of course, none of us had seen anything else
outside our home and so everything was new and strange. There
were really too few of us to decide who was 'different' and who
was not. We had so little information to go on. When Mother
returned no doubt, she would be able to explain everything,
besides there were our rapidly improving powers of sight and
hearing to amuse us.

It soon became quite clear to all of us that outside the entrance
to our home lay something bigger; much, much bigger.

The noises from out there were huge and sweeping. There were calls and screeches of things clearly alive like us and mighty sounds that seemed to be coming from everywhere at once.

At this point we had no names for these sounds and even less explanation for them. Hedgehogs measure time by the events that affect us. The sun rises, it sets, we get hungry, tired, and thirsty; sometimes we know that water is falling, sometimes it isn't but it all takes 'time.' This is how we knew that Mother would soon be home and, before long, she was.

The light in our nest dipped as Mother passed through the entrance. Mother looked like my sister and brothers but much, much bigger. But we were not at all surprised. Our eyes were only confirming what we had already felt and her presence was instantly comforting.

'Mother' my Sister called, 'I can see - and so can the Light One and we can all hear!'

Mother chuckled in the warm and reassuring way that only mothers can.

'Well well well, aren't we clever then?'

We all knew Mother by her scent and by the way she gently moved and nuzzled us, but this was the first time we had heard her voice; soft, warm, calm and comforting. It was a sound that would stay with us long after we had made our own ways in the world and would be a soothing memory during cold nights, lean times and scary encounters.

My powers of sight and hearing were getting better and better and after Mother had fed us and taken a long and well-earned sleep she awoke to groom and feed her hoglets. Afterwards she settled down and called us to attention.

'Now that you can all hear you can gather around, make yourselves comfortable, and listen to me. There is much you need to know.'

I could already tell my siblings from one another by their scents and the noises they made as they moved - and soon my sight would be good enough to distinguish them too, just as my sister already could. But Mother had decided it was time for us all to be made aware of our identities.

'Would you all like to know your names?' She asked.

'Names?' My brothers echoed in unison.

'Your names...' Mother explained, '...are what you are called. Names can be a scent or a noise. We are speaking to each other now - making noises that mean things. Names are like that. We can use them to tell others who we are or to remind us of our relatives. Everything must have a name, it would be impossible to share news and stories otherwise.'

'We are called Hedgehogs - all of us, that is the type of creature we are; there are many different types of creature, some tiny and some much, much bigger than us. Some are friendly, some are food - we eat them to survive, some are very dangerous and some we rarely see. You have much to learn.'

'So - our names?' My sister asked.

'Ah yes, your names,' Mother adjusted a pile of leaves and settled down a little more comfortably. 'Your Father might well have been called Rainpuddle, he was the handsomest hedgehog I ever met and so you two boys over here (She kissed each of my brothers on their noses) will be called Rain and Puddle.' My brothers began giggling;

'Pleased to meet you Rain!'

'Pleased to meet you too, Puddle!'

'And you, my only-daughter, I will name in memory of my own mother, she was called "Dawn", which is the name of the time when the sun rises in the sky to turn night into day.'

'Night into day?' I asked. So many of these words confused me, Mother chuckled.

'All in good time,' she said.

'Dawn - I like that' my sister sounded pleased.

'Hello Dawn' my brothers laughed and called.

'Hello Rain, hello Puddle' she answered politely.

'Now then,' Mother turned her attention to me. 'My rare and special boy - you shall be called, Northwind'.

The sound of my new name echoed in my head.

'Northwind.'

I must have looked confused. Rain and Puddle were happily calling to each other with their new names – but what did mine mean?

'I have called you Northwind because you are a very rare and special little hedgehog.'

'Why is HE special and not us?' Puddle sounded indignant.

Mother chuckled, 'You are all special to me, very special, but Northwind here - as you can all now probably see - is special in a different way.'

'Yes - but why?' Rain sounded confused. Mother turned to him.

'Night is dark, day is lighter; you know that night follows day, dark follows light? You've been around long enough to see it happening?'

We all agreed.

'But days and nights do not stay the same length. At this time, nights are short and getting shorter, there is more daylight and less and less darkness. There will come a night soon that will be the shortest night of all - and the longest day too. Then the reverse will start to happen. This is called 'The Seasons' and it repeats over and over again, forever.'

'Yes, but what is this to do with Northwind?' Puddle asked impatiently.

Mother laughed. 'I'm coming to that; so, when the days get shorter and the nights grow longer, it's as if the whole of the Great Outside needs to take a rest and everything starts to go to sleep before winter comes.'

There were lots of words we didn't understand but we politely kept silent, allowing Mother to continue her tale. No doubt it would all become clear as she went along.

'Winter is a season when the days are at their shortest and the nights are longest; but that's not all; it gets colder, much colder, and the wind - that's the great rush you hear shaking the trees - comes from a new direction; from the north, a north wind. And the north wind brings frost and snow that covers the land, freezing it and turning everything white.'

Mother's description of frost and snow as a great cold blanket made us all shiver, even though we were warm at that time in our home.

'White?' Now Dawn sounded puzzled.

'White...' explained Mother, '...is what you get when it is light but there are no other shades; just like little Northwind here. Snow and frost are so cold that all the other shades are frozen out of them and all that is left is white and the glittering silver of starlight; it makes the whole world twinkle.'

'It sounds pretty,' said Dawn.

'It is beautiful,' agreed Mother, 'but very dangerous. Hedgehogs can easily die in such cold and creatures made hungry by the cruel season hunt for anything they can eat to survive.'

We all shuddered. Mother continued.

'So that's why most hedgehogs do something special throughout the winter, we slow everything down and try to move as little as possible; our bodies do just enough to stop us from freezing and so they need only a tiny bit of food to keep going until the frost and snow has gone and the warmth and life returns to the Great Outside. You see, winter may be a harsh time, but it allows everything to rest and start again, refreshed and new.'

'And all of this is brought by the north wind?' I asked rather proudly.

Mother smiled. 'All brought by the north wind, yes;

But, my darling little boy, I'm afraid that being special comes at a high price. A beautiful thing is made to be seen - but for a hedgehog, being seen is not always a good thing.'

We must have looked puzzled because Mother sighed and continued. 'You know from your lessons that there are many different types of creature...?'

25

We all nodded.

'...and that some of them are food? We eat them to survive?'

We nodded again, this time a little more nervously.

'Well somewhere out there...' She glanced toward the entrance, '...are lots of different mothers telling their babies the very same thing...'

A sudden chill stole the warmth from our home, we looked fearfully from one to the other and it appeared that Rain and Puddle no longer envied my bright, white coat.

*   *   *

3

The Great Outside

Just as Mother predicted, there came a day longer than all the others and with it a night that was shorter.

For many days and nights, we had slept and grown while beyond our nest the summer sun blazed down and the countless creatures of the daytime had flown and scurried and walked and slithered and crawled and buzzed about their business.

Every evening, before Mother went out hunting, she would gather us around and tell us tales of the Great Outside, the creatures we shared it with and many things we would encounter when it was finally time for us to leave the safety of the only place we had known.

We were eager to experience it for ourselves and so were delighted one evening when Mother studied each of us in turn for longer than usual as if to help her come to a decision.

We could sense something special was going to happen. Rain and Puddle were almost bouncing up and down with excitement and even Dawn, usually so cool and calm, could hardly contain herself.

'It is time,' was all Mother said; and on this occasion, when she pushed her way through the exit from our home, we followed...

Both Rain and Puddle tried to get out at once and in their eagerness got stuck and had to come back in together to regroup. It was Dawn who led the four of us out and as she saw the great outside for the first time I heard her gasp.

'Ohhh, it's... it's...' She struggled to find the words.

'It's what? ...what?' Rain and Puddle were trying to nudge her out of the way so they too could exit. I was content to wait for the others to sort themselves out although I was as keen as anyone to see it all for myself.

There were gasps from up above as my brothers finally got a glimpse of what lay beyond our home. Suddenly they shot back through the entrance, squealing and grunting in shock.

'The... the roof... is too high!' squealed Rain.

'And... and the walls are so far away - so far away you can't see them!' Puddle exclaimed.

'Dawn and Mother are standing out there, looking up and all around,' Rain snorted in disbelief.

'And... the whole of the roof is black but there's a shining light right up above with nothing holding it there!' Puddle sounded completely baffled by his experience.

It was time to see all this for myself; the entrance to our nest had been a place of fascination ever since the power of sight had revealed it. Like a second birth it invited us to leave a familiar place for something new, a bigger place, a place to grow and learn.

It had silently called to us, inviting us on with the promise of something amazing.

And now, at last... out through

the entrance and...

'Ohhh!' There were no words in me to describe it.

Mother had told us what to expect but seeing it all for the very first time; the Great Outside; the huge sweep of night, the mighty sky, the countless twinkles glittering against blackness that went on forever; the moon was a big crescent hanging above the trees. There were so many different scents and calls of the other night creatures and, as I looked up in wonder, an owl glided silently above and disappeared into the distance across the fields.

'It's beautiful!' Dawn whispered.

'Yes, it is.' I agreed.

Rain and Puddle had got over their initial shock and were standing behind us.

'It's just so big,' said Rain.

'And... big.' Puddle could find no other words to describe how it all seemed to us little hoglets.

'Just a short walk,' Mother said and headed off away from our home. Nervously we followed.

Almost immediately it was clear how my appearance was going to present a problem.

Mother and my brothers and sister were very difficult to see as they moved through the grass and fallen twigs; they were as dark and shadowy as the world around them, while I seemed to shine out like a small drop of the moon that had fallen to Earth.

Our home was in the side of a small hill covered in grass and flowers. Behind our home, fields stretched away to a tall hedge and from beyond the hedge I could hear a growl that came and went accompanied by strange lights that moved as quickly as the owl that had crossed the dark sky a short time before.

Ahead of us, just across a narrow field, stood a wood, great trees swayed in the wind and between their trunks the night was at its darkest. From somewhere in that darkness the sound of unimaginable creatures made me instinctively fearful.

'We are not going into the wood tonight,' Mother reassured us. 'Just for a short walk along the side of this hill and then back home.'

And so, around the little hill we went, with Mother occasionally pausing to sniff the air and listen to the world and to allow us to catch up. Dawn followed her closest, followed by me, with Rain and Puddle bringing up the rear and arguing almost continuously about everything they saw, scented and heard.

'The little lights in the sky are the eyes of things watching us!' stated Rain confidently. 'They're bright and shiny like Northwind's eyes.'

'Nonsense' sniffed Puddle, 'Why would they watch us? I'll tell you what they are, they're bits of daylight that get left behind when the night comes, just like when Mother sweeps all the old leaves out of the home to make way for new ones. A few bits always get left behind.'

'If you two don't stop arguing, you'll be the ones left behind!' Dawn warned them.

'Ha ha - we can't get lost,' giggled Rain.

'No, we've got Northwind to follow and we can see him from a long way off!' added Puddle.

Mother called us together. 'It's not just about seeing; hedgehog vision is not good, there are lots of creatures out there whose eyes are much better than ours. It's about listening carefully, checking for scents and being aware of all that is around you. And mostly...' she eyed Rain and Puddle   '...It is about making as little noise as possible.'

Our walk continued with my two brothers still arguing, but now in whispers. There were so many things I wanted to know but Mother had told us to walk and look and listen and scent. She promised to answer all our questions as soon as we were safely back home.

So many questions...

This was the Great Outside, this was where we would hunt and be hunted and grow and hopefully meet a mate and have our own young. We needed to know as much as we could. There was so little time to learn it all.

One day soon we would be on our own; the thought scared me as we scurried along behind Mother. There was so much a hedgehog needed to know to survive out here and although it was all very exciting it was also a relief when we had skirted the whole of the little hill and once more reached the entrance to our home.

Inside now seemed so small but at the same time cosy and reassuring. It was good to be back and Mother was happy that the very first family walk had taken place without any problems. She needed to go back out there now to hunt but we had so many questions and were all speaking at once.

'What were those noises in the woods?'

'Did you sense that flying thing?'

'What are those growling, fast-moving lights?'

'When will we go out again?'

Mother chuckled. 'You are all home safe and sound and you will go out again when the next night comes. Now stay here and wait, all your questions will be answered when I return.'

And with a final chuckle she was back through the entrance and out into that great place of mystery and wonder.

And, as promised, she returned and fed us and slept then answered all our questions. When night fell again we returned to the great outside and walked around the little hill, this time stopping to listen out for strange new sounds and take in the scents.

We did this night after night; even the nights when it rained but, as hedgehogs hate rain, we used the shelter of bushes as much as we could. Even so, we experienced the sensation of getting wet and having to dry ourselves again.

We went out in the high winds and the quiet times and when there was a moon and when there was not and when the sky blazed with twinkles and when there was nothing above but clouds.

Then, one of us at a time went back out with Mother and she taught us how to hunt. We learned what we could eat and what to avoid. Without us realising it, Mother was helping us to become fully independent hedgehogs able to take care of ourselves.

Her lessons with me were a little different as she had to help me blend in to the countryside. She taught me to hide and to roll in leaves to help with camouflage and to keep perfectly still when I was unsure of any creature that came too close.

'All of us have to be careful but you, my darling Northwind, will always need to be very VERY careful.' she said kindly.

We started becoming impatient for nightfall so that we could explore and hunt with Mother before returning home, then she would leave again to hunt alone; afterwards would come the lessons and the questions.

It was a bright dawn on a day when the leaves were starting to change colour on the trees. We could hear the birds singing and chattering - so many different kinds - and in the distance the occasional roar of the great fast beasts with moons for eyes that Mother had warned us to avoid. We awoke surprised.

Usually we were up and about before daybreak so that Mother could bring us food before she rested, but no one had woken us, it was fully light outside and there was no sign of Mother.

'Maybe she has stopped for a rest after a really long walk?' suggested Rain.

'She was late once before after that storm when she had to avoid the mud and floodings, remember?' offered Puddle.

'But she was still back before it got fully light,' said Dawn.

Some little creatures have senses that no human can understand. Birds can fly great distances and land in the same spot each year and some animals flee when they know something really bad is coming - long before it happens.

Suddenly, it felt as if winter had arrived inside me. It was a deep and frightening cold just as if the sun had gone from the sky. It was clear from Dawn's nervousness that she knew it too. We shared an awful and terrifying realisation.

Mother wasn't coming home.

*   *   *

4

Food & Drink

The sun rose higher. We were tired and hungry but afraid to sleep.

'She has to come back!' stated Rain.

'She has to,' repeated Puddle.

'...She loves us; she wouldn't leave us.'

'Boys... listen to me.'

We had all come to respect Dawn, she was the calmest and most level-headed of us all and it was our clever sister we turned to now for reassurance.

'Northwind understands - and so do I - and I know you both understand as well but it's just too painful to admit it. Mother has gone.'

'No!' Rain cried; '...don't say that.'

'She's right Rain,' I said, 'it's time to be strong now and remember all she taught us.'

Puddle was crying too but trying really hard to be brave. 'We will - we'll be good hedgehogs and take care of each other, just like she would have wanted.'

We all started crying then but sometimes that is a good thing because it can help to wash away grief and do what needs to be done.

'Yes,' Dawn said, 'We will be good hedgehogs and take care of each other, and the first thing we need to do is find food and drink.'

It helped us all to have something to do and something to concentrate on.

'We can't go out there in the daylight.' Puddle stated.

'We must, we have to drink and find some food,' said Rain.

'I will go.' I heard myself say.

'No Northwind, it's too dangerous, we will have to wait until it is dark.' said Dawn.

We all knew; however, that in the warmth of our home we would be terribly thirsty by the time night came.

'That will be too long,' I argued, 'I will find something to drink close by and come back and lead us to it; it's the only way. We know that after it has rained there is water at the edge of the field - Mother's Pool remember? And it rained a lot yesterday.'

'Twice the ears and twice the noses are safer, I'm coming with you,' said Dawn, '...You boys wait here and we'll be back.'

Rain and Puddle huddled together for comfort, they looked so unhappy it was hard leaving them but it was important that we found drink and food.

At the top of the tunnel where the sun had beaten down all day the earth was warm beneath my feet. There was no breeze to disturb the grasses that surrounded the entrance and a fat bee, startled by our approach, lifted slowly into the air and buzzed away. Dawn and I passed through into a world quite unlike the one we had experienced with Mother.

The light hurt my eyes; Dawn was squinting as we slowly waited to adjust to the unfamiliar daytime. The Great Outside seemed like a completely different place now. The air was full of the chatter of birds and the woods, so dark and fearful at night, were many different shades.

The field was very different too and the sky above was pale and light. We had no names for all these different shades then - except for one. The flowers on our little hill were... white! The same as me.

The sun was warm on my back and busy insects buzzed around me, hovering to get a better look, as we skirted around the side of the hill in the direction of the great field.

Sure enough, there was the large puddle of water at the edge of the field where it looked as if the earth had been worn away by something we couldn't imagine. I drank my fill while Dawn kept watch then we switched over.

'Go home now, take extra care, and tell Rain and Puddle to come to Mother's Pool. I will wait here for them under the thorny bush.' Dawn ordered.

The trail back to our home was now well-known to us all and my waiting brothers were told where they would find a drink - and to keep quiet along the way! The nest seemed so empty with just me in it. During daylight hours we had always had the comforting presence of our sleeping mother and now she was no longer there.

The air inside was stuffy and warm compared to the Great Outside and the smells which had once been so comforting saddened me in my loneliness. The scent of Mother still hovered all around but was now surprisingly painful because of her absence.

Being there alone was just unbearable and so I set back out to follow Rain and Puddle and met them as they were returning.

'Dawn is still at Mother's Pool...,' Rain announced, '...looking for worms.'

'Yes, we said we could look too but she said we would be safer at home,' stated Puddle with some disappointment.

'Perhaps she's right,' I agreed. 'It might not be safe for all of us to be out together in the daylight. I'll go and find her and bring her home.'

Rain and Puddle scurried off in the direction of our home leaving me to skirt the hill from where it was possible to see Mother's Pool at the edge of the field. I almost bumped into my sister coming the other way carrying a worm.

'Itff only one mmbut we can fare ih,' she mumbled before putting the worm down and holding it in place with her foot. 'Sorry, I meant to say, it's only one but we can share it.'

'You're a good hunter Sister,' it was hard not to be impressed with her prowess.

'Mother taught us well,' she smiled sadly and, picking up the worm, followed me back to our home.

Having eaten and drank we were overcome with tiredness and so we slept. My sleep was filled with dazzling dreams of Mother and of the dazzling daytime and of things with no words to describe them. I awoke before the others to find the sun had gone down behind the trees; Dawn, her voice still full of sleep, called to me as I was about to disappear through the entrance.

'Northwind, where are you going?'

'I am going to get a drink and try to hunt.' I whispered, trying not to wake Rain and Puddle.

'Take care, and don't go too far,' she murmured.

Night was falling; the sky behind the woods was becoming a deep pool of darkness and the air was full of the calls of birds arguing and discussing where they were going to sleep. I crept nervously around the little hill and looked down to Mother's Pool. All seemed peaceful and the drink on arriving was cool and welcome.

Hedgehogs are not picky, we will eat pretty much anything but, as the world got darker - I did not! And the darker it became the more I seemed to shine out. The only thing to do was to head back to our home. There was an idea forming that went against all that hedgehogs are supposed to do but when you are a special hedgehog you need a special plan. Dawn would know if my idea was a good one or not.

There was movement in the field behind me. From a vantage point at the top of our little hill it was clear to see... a creature, it had to be, and much bigger than a hedgehog. It stopped, raised its head as if to scent and then trotted on again. It was heading toward Mother's Pool.

There are many strange scents around the pool and Mother had warned us to be extra careful there. All creatures need to drink and so it could be a place of danger.

There are large clumps of long grass on the far side of our hill and I crept among them and tried to keep perfectly still, hoping the creature would go on its way and not follow my path or discover my scent.

To head home when your scent is being followed is to put everyone in danger.

The wait seemed to last forever. It was quite dark now and if, as Mother had warned us, many creatures' sight was keen and sharp, it would see anything that moved out there.

A sudden shout from right behind me made me jump off on all four feet at once and squeal with shock.

'Hey, Northwind - I caught a snail!' Puddle came crashing through the twigs closely followed by Rain, '...and I got a centipede - big one as well!'

I cringed, 'Ssshhhhh!'

Then they saw the creature too.

It was padding around on the edge of the field; it would walk quickly for a small distance in one direction, then sniff the air, then turn around and follow a new path as if searching for the origin of a particularly interesting scent.

'I don't like the look of it, not at all,' Rain was shivering as he whispered.

'We should get home as quickly as we can and warn Dawn not to come out,' said Puddle.

'No,' I stated, 'If we run for it now we might... *I* might... be seen and that could lead the creature to our home. You two creep carefully back; go on, I'll stay hidden for a while and watch.'

Rain and Puddle exited the bush from behind and crept slowly home on a route where the grass was longest. Looking down towards the field, the creature was still sniffing the air. As long as the pair took care and remembered all that Mother had taught them they were going to be safe and our home would stay undetected.

There followed another long wait before daring to look again, as I peered out a strange small voice from behind startled me.

'Be it still sniffing about out there?'

It was a small, thin and completely new voice that appeared to be coming from nowhere, but then, peering from behind a thick clump of grass, two sharp black eyes looked me up and down curiously; a set of twitching whiskers seemed to be gathering information about me and our surroundings.

'Yes... I mean, yes it is... and who... what... are you?'

'I'm a wood mouse, my name be Patience; haven't you seen a mouse before?'

'Actually, no; I'm rather new to all of this,' I answered politely.

'What be you?' the little mouse asked me.

'I'm a hedgehog of course, are you new at all of this too?'

The little mouse chuckled nervously, 'No, I've been around since before last winter and I've seen me a hedgehog lots of times. Of course, I try to avoid them, especially if they look hungry, but you be very small for a hedgehog - be you male or female? I'm female. How is it that you be white? I'll bet your name is Snow or Frost or something?'

'It's Northwind and I be, I mean I am... male - and we should be keeping quiet.'

I decided to take another look and popped my head out of the long grass under the bush.

'Come back in,' whispered Patience, 'I be much harder to spot and my eyesight be better than yours, let me see what I can see.'

Patience crept past me and stood on her hind legs for a better view, her head turned this way and that and she stretched her neck to make sure she missed nothing.

'I can't see it - I think it's gone,' she whispered.

With relief I prepared to move out and head off on my way when the bush rustled loudly behind me and the air was full of a sudden hot breath. Patience turned and looked up, horror-stricken; I also turned and found myself facing the biggest teeth I had ever seen and a pair of very intelligent glittering eyes.

'Who are we hiding from?' The creature asked with a terrifying smile.

*   *   *

5

Flame

With the tiniest of squeaks, Patience fell over in a faint and I froze to the spot as the creature studied me.

An older and more experienced hedgehog would have immediately curled into a ball but when you are that frightened it's sometimes impossible to move at all.

The creature licked its lips and put its head to one side; when it spoke, there was music in the voice, a pleasant lilt and the feeling that laughter was never far away. But it was still terrifying.

'What in the Great Outside are you?'

I tried to reply but all that came out was a tiny grunt.

It moved its nose so close it was almost touching me and took a good sniff.

'I thought I had seen every creature there was - but I've never seen one like you before!' it stated.

My voice, when it eventually came out, sounded almost as tiny as that of Patience,

'I'm... I'm a hedgehog.'

There was a short silence followed by a sudden loud laugh. The creature's fearsome teeth shone as white as my coat in the light of the moon that had begun to rise above the trees.

'A hedgehog? A HEDGEHOG? Don't make me laugh. I know what a hedgehog looks like - I should do, I've eaten enough of them!'

The revelation caused me to shudder as the creature continued, '...You're sort of the same shape as a hedgehog, but smaller, and you're...'

'White, yes,' I interrupted, '...but I'm still a hedgehog - just an unusual one.'

It took a step backwards and the thought of running briefly crossed my mind, but it was clear I wouldn't get far. With a tiny groan Patience was regaining consciousness.

'Ohhh,' she squeaked, 'Be I still alive?'

She caught sight of the creature and started trembling. Closing her eyes, she shrank into the grass as if to try and disappear from its view.

'For all I know you could be poisonous...,' the creature said, '...maybe that's why you look so funny. Now that's good news for you because it means I'm not going to risk eating you - besides I'm full up, I've already had my evening meal and couldn't face another mouthful. In fact...' the creature put its nose right up to Patience and whispered in mock menace, '...I doubt I could even fit a mouse in!'

Patience opened one eye, saw how close the creature was, and closed it again, her whiskers trembled. From somewhere I found the courage to speak, I thought that if this fearsome creature was going to eat us, it may have done so by now - and I was curious.

'Please creature... what are you?'

The creature looked at me in surprise.

'What am I? WHAT AM I?'

It stood up at full height causing me to shuffle backwards; it shook its head and fixed me with a gaze full of both surprise and amusement.

'Don't you get out much?' It asked.

'Excuse me,' interrupted Patience, 'He be very young, he'd never seen a mouse before.'

'Really?' The creature sounded amazed, 'Don't know much about anything then, do you?'

It must have looked a sorry sight; a tiny, strange wintry little hedgehog wondering if it was about to end up as someone's supper on its very first hunt.

'Well...' the creature began importantly, '...I am a fox - and a rather handsome one. I'm also very clever - in fact, I'm the cleverest creature you'll ever meet. Go on, ask me a question, anything... there's not much we foxes don't know. My name is Flame, named after my father - I got my good looks from him too, and my intelligence... and courage. Luckily for you I got kindness and self-control from my mother.'

'I'm pleased to meet you,' I replied politely.

'Oh yes? You'd be the first hedgehog that ever was!' Flame gave another loud and musical laugh.

Introductions seemed the polite thing to do.

'My name is Northwind and this is Patience.' the little mouse tried to smile but was clearly still terrified.

For a moment the fox looked at me, eyes wide, then he growled loudly and angrily, pawing the ground in some sort of inner rage; he turned away, growled again then fixed his gaze back on me.

'Great steaming buck-rabbits and hare's bums, that's blown it!' He roared angrily, '...Now I couldn't eat you even if I wanted to!'

His reaction was utterly confusing.

What could be annoying about someone's name?

'What's the matter? I'm sorry if I have said the wrong thing, I was just trying to be polite. I've never met a fox before, although Mother told me about them.'

Mentioning Mother filled me with a sudden dread; could this fox have...?

'...Actually, I haven't seen my Mother for two nights and I feel as if she's gone; did you, by any chance...?'

Flame shook his head. 'Eh? No... no, not me - haven't eaten a hedgehog for... oh, a long time - and now I can't eat you - or Squeaky Twitchy Whiskers over there. You see, my mother told me never to eat something if I knew its name, that way I'll never eat my friends by mistake. Silly I call it but mothers are usually right. Now my father on the other hand, he would eat anything, he ate a human's dinner once; the fools left it unguarded in a house and he, bold as anything, wandered in and ate it - and then did a poo in their garden before leaving! What a fox!' Flame laughed loudly.

'He sounds very brave,' Patience said.

'Brave? I should say so, that's where I get it from, I'm afraid of nothing me - and I'm clever, did I tell you that? The cleverest creature you'll ever meet.'

'Yes, yes you did,' I confirmed.

'Right, well...' Flame sniffed the air, 'Can't hang around all night talking to frosty-faced hedgehogs and squeaky snacks, there's a pretty young lady fox somewhere around here that I'd rather like to meet up with; her name's Fern - same as my mother, so... must fly, good hunting North Star - and watch out for my father!'

With a bound, Flame was off at high speed out across the narrow field in the direction of the woods.

'It's Northwind - and... thank you for not eating us.' I called after him, but he was already out of sight.

I caught my first worm sometime during that night. The moon had travelled across the sky and was lowering toward the human nest beyond the place where the Moon-Eyed Beasts roamed. I offered to share it with Patience who had insisted on following me around, but she declined, saying she knew of a delicious berry bush she would be visiting on her way home at sunrise.

'I'm surprised you didn't say thank you to the worm,' Patience was following me down a narrow track that would, if my memory served me well, lead us back to the edge of the field close to Mother's Pool from where home was just a short walk.

'What do you mean?' I was only half-listening; Patience had proved to be a chatty little mouse and throughout the night had told me all about her many relatives and where she lived and what mice do and don't do.

'Well,' she said, 'I know you have to eat, but worms be living things - berries too by the way - and it's just manners to thank them for feeding you.'

'Do you say thank you to berries?' It sounded an odd thing to do.

'Of course,' she replied, '...and I'm sure Flame would have thanked us if he had eaten us. You are only young so perhaps you haven't realised but all the lives depend on all the other lives. Always remember - every life matters - that's what my mother used to say. Yes, every life matters. I had five brothers and sisters you know, then another five, then six, then another five!'

Just before sunrise, Patience ate a caterpillar and thanked it. The night had been long and home was calling.

'Maybe I'll be seeing you tonight?' Patience said as our paths parted.

'Yes, maybe' I agreed and headed around the little hill for home. There was much to tell my sister and brothers, and much to warn them about.

Dawn, Rain and Puddle were asleep. Mother had told us about foxes, she had said they were very dangerous to hedgehogs and unpredictable and that they were also very clever.

Flame had seemed all of those things and Patience, while talkative, had been an interesting companion who had lived through a winter and had told me lots about the big white blanket that covered the world and the long sleep that some creatures took until everything came back to life.

I was going to suggest to Dawn that, because of my bright white coat it might be safer to hunt in the evening light or early mornings as it was just too easy to see me in the dark. She seemed to have remembered everything Mother had ever said to us and so she would know whether it was a good idea or not.

My adventures and encounters would just have to wait, even though I was bursting with news. Finally, a deep drowsiness came and while the sun passed across the sky of the Great Outside there would be dreams of mice and foxes. Just before sleep finally claimed me, I remembered to murmur a 'thank you' to a worm whose name I never knew.

*   *   *

6

Do Not Even Think of Running

I woke to an empty nest having slept all through the hours of daylight. It was already dark outside and Dawn, Rain and Puddle had clearly gone out hunting. This was to become the way of things.

Very early in the lives of hedgehogs we tend to head off on our different paths until we usually lose touch with each other completely.

There was so much to tell my siblings about my adventures of the night before and my plans to go hunting before darkness fell, but there was nothing to be done for it now; first there was the need to eat and drink. It had been a warm day and on scuttling out into the night a cool breeze felt refreshing.

There were twinkles overhead but the moon had not yet risen. From a distance across the big field came the occasional roar of a Moon-Eyed Beast as it rushed along about its unknown business.

Pausing to sniff the air revealed nothing of concern although many of the scents were still of creatures unknown to me. A drink was the first thing needed and so Mother's Pool was my first destination.

Flame the Fox had not eaten me and it was clear this was a rare and lucky thing to happen - but there were no guarantees in the

Great Outside. If we met again - and he was hungry enough - the outcome might be different. But Patience the Wood Mouse had survived for a long time out here so at least it was possible with planning and wisdom.

There was surprisingly little water in Mother's Pool. Of course, there had been no rain and it had been a hot day but none of us could remember the pool ever being dry.

It worried me that, if there should be no rain for many days, there would be no water here at all, then where would we drink? Mother probably knew many other places - but Mother was gone.

This called for some exploring, but first came a drink from what was left of the pool and then it was time to skirt the edge of the field where the grass was long to see what was on the far side of the hill. It might not be a good idea to spend too much time on this edge of the field because this was where Flame had been patrolling the night before.

I walked quite a long way around the field, pausing every now and again to rest, scent and listen. It was during one of these pauses that there came a noise up ahead; just a small noise but a familiar one. Venturing forward, I gave off a series of reassuring grunts to announce my approach.

Sure enough, a familiar face popped up from the long grass, it was my sister, Dawn.

'Northwind,' she smiled, 'We thought you were going to sleep all night as well as all day.'

She had just caught a slug and generously shared it with me which gave me the chance to tell her all about my adventures from the night before.

'You must have been terrified..,' she looked shocked at my close encounter, '...but it could have been much worse, it could have been a badger.'

'I thought it was at first,' I explained, 'I couldn't recall everything Mother told us about their appearance; all I remember her saying was something about great big teeth and Flame certainly had those.'

Dawn thought my idea of hunting in the half light of evening and early morning was worth a try and might give me a better chance of remaining hidden from those who did not have Flame's restraint and who would not care at all what my name was.

We hunted together all night until the sun began to lighten the sky beyond the woods.

To the far side of the wood a ribbon of mist was forming, it seemed to curve around the edge of the trees and away towards the horizon.

'We need to find somewhere else to drink,' I told Dawn; 'I don't think Mother's Pool is going to last much longer without rainfall.'

My sister just smiled as she watched the mist forming, I watched it too.

'It's pretty,' I said.

'Yes, isn't it...,' she agreed, '...It was her name you know.'

I must have looked confused.

'Her name, Brother, it was Mother's name - she was called Rivermist; she told me once as we stood just here and watched the mist forming. Rivermist always comes just after dawn - and her mother had been called Dawn, which is why she gave the name to me.'

'If I should ever have hoglets, I'm going to call one of them Rivermist. Look Northwind, the mist is rising off the river and that is where we can drink - always. You see, even though Mother has gone it's as if she is still guiding us.'

We walked back around to our own side of the hill, confident now that there would always be water to drink. Even though I had not remembered everything Mother had taught me, enough had been hopefully stored away to keep me safe while exploring the Great Outside and all the amazing things in it.

There was no sign of Rain or Puddle at the nest when we returned home. We were not too concerned, it was even possible they had found somewhere to make a home of their own, hedgehogs regularly change their nests, but they were still in the area as we had both scented them in the night.

It was only a matter of time before we bumped into them somewhere.

I awoke in the evening, but it was still quite light. Dawn was asleep and so I quietly left our home and skirted the hill to get a view of the wide field. Birds were circling overhead; I could hear their calls but understood little of their complicated language. Mother had told us birds had their own language but that some of them understood ours too.

The air was full of scents, some were familiar and some strange. Many more creatures were out and about in the daylight and for my plan to work there was much to learn to become familiar with them.

'You be up early!'

The small voice was just behind me and the tiny twitching nose of Patience appeared out of a clump of dandelions.

'I do wish you wouldn't sneak up on me, you gave me a fright,' I told her.

'Sorry,' she said, 'But when you be a mouse it pays to be very quiet - as 'quiet as a mouse' some creatures say.'

'Yes, well perhaps, but could you at least approach me from the front?'

'I'll try,' Patience laughed, 'I see you be out in the daylight instead of the night - good plan.'

'Do you really think so?' I asked.

'Oh yes, you be too easy to spot in the dark but now, if you were to stand among a bunch of daisies, I'd hardly know you were there.' Patience paused to nibble on a couple of seeds that had fallen from a bush.

I caught a delicious black beetle and after eating it remembered to say 'Thank You' which Patience seemed pleased about.

'Have you seen Flame around?' I asked her.

'No, thank goodness,' she shuddered, 'I had daymares after that.'

'He seemed friendly enough to me,' I offered.

Patience frowned.

'Everyone be friendly on a full stomach, Northwind, but remember; if two hungry creatures miss one meal they will share the next one, if they miss two they will fight over it and if they miss three meals they will try to eat each other.'

'I suppose being a mouse, you see things a bit differently,' I said to her.

'Yes, perhaps,' she said, but her mind was elsewhere, she had spotted an inviting berry bush and she scurried into the grass towards it.

Almost immediately she reversed back out at top speed, whiskers quivering and her tiny body trembling. Her little black eyes were full of terror and she stared as if hypnotised back into the long grass.

'Patience...? What's the...?'

'Ssssh!' She whispered, her tiny voice full of fear. 'Don't make any sound Northwind and keep still - keep very still!'

I did as she asked; peering into the grass to see what had terrified her.

The grass began to rustle and suddenly filled with a completely alien scent. My instinct was to scurry away as fast as possible, but if my little friend's advice was good then staying rooted to the spot was wisest. There was not long to wait for my curiosity to be answered.

The face that rose from the surrounding grass was unlike any I had seen before, but it was full of menace. The eyes were unblinking and a thin tongue flicked in and out as a head swayed a little on a long neck.

What was it that Mother had told me about a creature that looked like this? Dawn would remember if she were here. Patience was frozen to the spot at my side, she had looked afraid when confronted by Flame but now it seemed as if she knew this was her last day and that scared me more than anything. When the creature spoke, it was as if its words had formed from the wind.

'Do not even think of running, I can strike faster than you can move!'

* * *

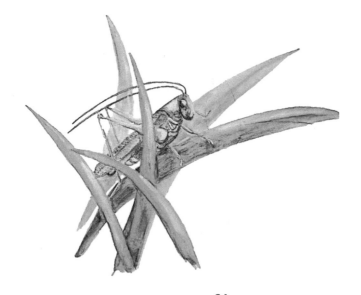

7

Everything Is Afraid of Me

The thing watched, and even though it was a completely new creature to me the terrible power of it was clear. My mind was racing, what was it that Mother had taught us?

We had been so tired and ready for sleep. I wished my wise sister were here but then it was also a relief that she wasn't in this danger. Patience had passed beyond fear and now looked calm and accepting as if she knew her fate was decided.

The air was suddenly still, the breeze had dropped and the strange scent of this thing was all around us. It swayed, and its graceful but terrifying head moved between Patience and I as if choosing which of us would be getting its attention. Flame's eyes had been full of curiosity and intelligence - and even humour, but the eyes surveying us now were cold, pitiless and unblinking.

'I am called Northwind,' I said, hoping that knowing my name would offer the same protection it had with Flame.

How could any creature remain so completely still? It was as if time had stopped. A cricket balancing on a nearby blade of grass paused in mid-chirrup as if suddenly realising whose company it was in; and then it disappeared with a jump faster than my eye could follow. The strange and graceful head lowered and floated close to me.

'I don't care who you are,' it whispered, 'I'm more interested in... WHAT you are?'

My appearance had clearly confused it and once again the rarity of my whiteness, which Mother said would make life so difficult for me, may well have saved me - at least for a moment.

And then it all came back - Mother's lesson - and when I spoke much of my fear had gone!

'I am... a hedgehog!'

There was no emotion in the creature's face, the cold stare continued but I could sense intelligence now and it seemed to be swaying from side to side a little more as if trying to get a better look at me.

'A hedgehog? Now you come to mention it, you do look like a *sort* of hedgehog, but a very strange one - not a proper hedgehog at all.'

I tried to make myself look as large as possible, which was difficult for such a young hoglet.

'Well I am a proper hedgehog - and you cannot hurt me and I'm not afraid of you!'

'Fool!' the creature hissed. 'Everything is afraid of me; foxes, badgers, horses, cattle, cats, dogs... even humans! Isn't that true... mouse?'

Patience nodded quickly, she looked as if she was going to faint. Many of those creature names were new to me, but if foxes and badgers - and even humans - were afraid of this thing, it must be very dangerous indeed.

The creature moved gracefully through the grass and looked at me from several different angles. I remained still.

'Let me guess,' the creature hissed and there was a trace of cruel amusement in its voice, 'Your mother - or someone equally misinformed - has told you not to be afraid of a certain something's bite because it can't hurt you... am I right?'

'Yes - and Mother was wise, you can't hurt me!' There must have been a hint of uncertainly in my voice as the creature sounded even more amused by my statement.

'Well there's one way to decide if your mother was correct isn't there?' it whispered right in my ear...

'I can bite you - and if you're still alive a short time later, she is as wise as you say; and if not, she is the fool I know her to be. Shall we try?'

'How about I bite you and see if you enjoy it?'

I was angry that the creature had called Mother a fool and it caused me to sound much braver than I actually felt. Patience looked at me as if I had lost my senses.

When the creature laughed it was like the sound of a sharp breeze blowing through the leaves of young trees. Without warning it struck at me and there wasn't even time to blink.

It stopped, its mouth wide open with the tip of my nose inside it. Two terrible-looking fangs dropped forward from the roof of its mouth, thin, deadly and sharper than any hedgehogs' spines. Terrified, I screwed up my eyes really tight and trembled, regretting my earlier bravado. But then, to my surprise the creature pulled back its head and closed its mouth. The head moved around to my ear and the creature whispered coldly.

'How about I don't bite you - how about... I crush you instead?'

I had gone beyond fear and now foolishly felt I had nothing to lose.

'It will be the most painful crush you have ever crushed.' I promised, 'My spines are the sharpest hedgehog spines in the Great Outside - and you can leave my little friend alone as well. If you make her your supper, I will make you mine!'

The creature laughed once more and lowered its head close to mine, 'Northwind' it said, its voice sounding just like I imagined the north wind itself would sound, 'I am called Sunn, I am an adder, and you are the only creature in the whole of the Great Outside who has ever dared speak to me like that.'

Mother had always told us to be respectful to everything we met and I regretted having been so rude.

'I'm sorry, I did not wish to be impolite; but I am frightened, I have never met an... adder before and you look so fierce.'

'Fierce? I'm not fierce,' Sunn sounded surprised, 'I'm one of the gentlest creatures you'll ever meet, but even I have to eat. I dare say there are things out there who think you are fierce - some might even find the little mouse fierce. I am actually very shy.'

Patience had started to calm down but was still on her guard. 'Oh no, not me, I'm not fierce at all,' she managed to say.

'Really? Tell that to the next caterpillar you eat, I'm sure they'll feel a lot better about being your breakfast,' Sunn hissed. 'Now, if you don't mind, I'm trying to sleep.'

'I'm sorry we disturbed you,' I informed the adder.

'Yes, well I'm sorry if I scared you. Ten winters I've survived - ten, and in all that time I've never seen such a wintry-looking hedgehog as you.'

I was aware of the sounds of the Great Outside returning as my panic eased.

'I'm very young; I haven't seen a winter yet.'

'Well, take it from me - winter looks just like you. In fact, I thought that was what you were, a little piece of winter that got left behind. Still, you're a very polite young hedgehog so as a special favour; I won't eat the mouse... today.'

'Thank you,' said Patience, still trembling, 'Come on Northwind, let's leave her in peace.'

'Her?' For some reason I had thought Sunn was a male.

'That's right, I'm a "Her"...' Sunn confirmed, '...now scuttle off and find some slugs or berries or whatever you prickly and furry things eat. Oh - and mothers may be wise, but they don't always know everything. Many summers past, a hungry hedgehog tried to eat me as I was sleeping; he actually bit me; I bit him back, he died. Have a nice day!'

'She was getting cold, that's what it was.'

Patience was trying to keep up with me as we tried to put as much distance as possible between us and Sunn. She chatted away busily as we walked.

'Yes, adders need warm sunshine; if they get cold they can't move as quickly,' she said.

'It moved quickly enough for me...,' I said, shuddering, '...and those fangs were almost touching the tip of my nose.'

'One of my brothers was eaten by an adder I think,' Patience explained, 'Not sure what his name was, I have so many brothers and sisters it's hard to remember them all.'

'I have two brothers, I haven't seen them for days,' I said, wondering just where Rain and Puddle were. Had they encountered such dangerous creatures as Flame and Sunn? I hoped they were safe and happy.

It was getting darker which made me easier to see although there was no moon and the twinkles were hidden behind brooding clouds. Unless it rained tonight we would probably have to go all the way to the river to get a drink the next time out.

'I'm tired and it's getting too dark for safety, I'm off back to my home soon,' I told Patience. She showed me where a thicket of brambles had lain mostly undisturbed and we shared a last meal of blackberries.

'I must say, it be very odd to see a hedgehog out in the light and going home at night - but I think you are wise to do so.' Patience had stuffed her cheeks with so much blackberry I could hardly understand her.

'I think it's for the best until I know more about the Great Outside, I've already had more scares than I care for.' I replied.

'Well you're probably right,' Patience agreed, 'I'm heading off to my burrow too, better safe than sorry, it's been a strange old day and if I never see another adder it will be too soon!'

Dawn had already gone out hunting when I arrived back at our home and there was no sign or scent of Rain or Puddle, they clearly hadn't been around for a while. I couldn't sleep, hedgehogs are nocturnal, we are designed to sleep in the day and hunt at night and it was going to take a bit of practise to get used to my upside-down way of doing things; instead, curling up in a warm pile of leaves and closing my eyes allowed my mind to drift off on journeys of its own.

What did it mean to be a part of this big amazing place... the Great Outside?

It was as if all the creatures fitted together and were part of a huge and complicated family - even the ones like Sunn, who appeared so unusual. What could it all mean? Maybe, as Patience had told me, 'every life matters' and we all needed each other.

Somewhere outside there was the call of what I now knew was an owl; I hoped Patience was in hiding. Poor little Patience, she must be such a clever mouse to have lived so long when it seemed everything was trying to eat her.

Were there any creatures out there that were not being hunted by something? Of course not, what a thought, what would be the point of them if nothing ate them? There was so much to learn. Sleep overtook me and when my eyes opened again Dawn was snoring away next to me and the sun was rising beyond the entrance to our nest.

Had it rained?

*   *   *

8

A Fox Is Coming!

Despite a few fat drops of rain there had been no real downpour. Outside a new and different breeze blew over the field... colder, shaking the bushes and bending the grass before it.

Heavy dark clouds rushed across the sky and birds shouted to each other as they were tossed around like the many leaves that had joined them to dance in the air.

Flattening my spines, I shuddered. No rain meant a journey to the river. Dawn was sleeping, she would be going out later and so, leaving quietly, I weaved my way down through the long grass of our little hill.

My journey was going to take me closer to the woods than ever before. But drinking was vital so there was no other way. I needed to get to the river and then back from the brooding trees before darkness fell.

This part of the Great Outside was no longer strange to me. My own travels as well as many stories from Patience and Dawn had made me familiar with the area we call home. Like all hedgehogs I can travel a great distance in a night, which is important if you must fill your stomach twice over every time you hunt.

The nest where we were born is in the side of a small hill near to a bush with white flowers growing on it which give off a pleasant scent especially in the mornings. The entrance faces a narrow field looking towards a wood. Around the side of this wood a river runs away into the distance.

Behind the woods, there are far distant hills according to Patience although I have never seen them; her eyesight is much better than mine. Walking around to the side of our hill leads to a bigger and wider field and on the far edge of it there is a long straight line of tall bushes.

Behind that line of bushes is the trail used by the Moon-Eyed Beasts which - so Patience was once told - are creatures who always live with humans and without humans to guide them, they cannot move.

Beyond their trail the ground rises in a larger hill with a sloping field at the bottom and more woods above. In a corner of that field is one of the big stone nests that humans build.

Mother told us that, while humans are strange and perform acts that make no sense, they will not usually harm hedgehogs - but they often share their nests with creatures that do.

The most dangerous of all these creatures is called a 'Flame Beast' - it has no face; it gets bigger and bigger by eating everything that comes near to it.

It even eats the clear air and blows out air you cannot breathe or see through. Its body keeps changing shape and it can light up the night sky.

I have never seen one of these creatures, but I have scented it and seen its breath dancing like baby rainclouds.

Sometimes, if you choose to sleep near a human nest this creature will suddenly appear all around you and make you so hot you will disappear and it will turn you into a part of itself.

I reached the bottom of our hill and set out across the narrow field that would take me to the river at the edge of the woods. In a tall bush two birds as dark as night sat on one of the branches. The shape of their beaks told me they were not the type who would regard a live hedgehog as food and so I offered a polite 'Good evening,' on passing.

'Whjarrr! Winterbright he be, skyfella coo like.' The one called harshly to his friend.

'Ha - Spiner foodsoon,' the other replied.

There was little time to stop for a conversation, but I thought it good manners to explain who and what I was.

'My name is Northwind; I am a hedgehog - a white hedgehog.'

One of the birds fluttered down from the branch and stood close to me, studying me with sharp and intelligent eyes, its head turned from side to side and it spoke very slowly as if trying to help me understand their strange speech.

'We call you Spiner... spines on body see? Why you white? Fool thing be white ground dark - foodsoon.'

I was about to reply when the bird's companion shouted from its branch.

'Sky sky! Rax come SKY!'

The bird at my side rose urgently into the sky screaming to me as he climbed, 'Rax come! Run Spiner!'

'Wait,' I called out, 'I don't understand what you're saying?'

However, there was no mistaking the voice that came from right behind me.

'Rax - it's their word for fox, they were warning you a fox was coming - and a jolly handsome one too!'

'Flame!' He had approached silently and now sat and sniffed the air.

'Isn't it amazing,' he said, 'We can spend generations not seeing a white hedgehog and then I bump into one twice in a matter of days. You're still alive, I am surprised. Where's the squeaky snack?'

'Patience? I haven't seen her since last night. Errr - have you eaten?' I enquired nervously.

Flame yawned and sniffed the air, 'Awfully kind of you to ask, but yes, I had a duck earlier.'

'Duck?' I enquired.

Flame shook his head at me, 'You really should get out more. Duck, a swimming birdie thing, annoyingly loud creatures, well, at least they are until you eat them!'

I was curious.

'Did you thank it?'

'I would have - but I couldn't get a word in... QUACK QUACK QUACK! I hate noisy food, don't you?'

I was still very much on my guard, reminding myself this was a fox, and even though he seemed friendly enough he was still a fox; clever, unpredictable and quite capable of eating me if he was hungry enough.

'I'm going to the river to drink,' I told him.

'Yes? Well I'll dawdle along with you for a while then but try and make those little legs go as fast as you can, I haven't got all night,' Flame replied with what I hoped was a smile.

He padded slowly beside me, 'Has your mother turned up yet?' he asked.

'No, I don't think she's coming back,' I replied sadly.

'Shame,' Flame replied, 'Mothers are so full of wisdom - "Remember Flame," my mother says, "you can learn something from every creature you meet." And she's right of course. I learned from you that hedgehogs come in interesting colours and that they are fascinating to have a conversation with - you're the first hedgehog I've ever talked to, do you know that?'

'Thank you,' I replied, 'It's nice talking to you too.'

'Yes,' Flame continued, '...and I learned from that duck just how tasty ducks are!' He laughed his musical laugh again. 'Clever fox, my mother, that's where I get it from. Did I tell you? I'm the cleverest creature you'll ever meet!'

'Yes, you did,' I replied politely, 'Oh, and I met an adder yesterday.'

Flame stopped in his tracks and studied me with sudden curiosity.

'Did you? Did you really?'

'I did,' I confirmed.

'Some say adder bites don't harm hedgehogs, others say that's nonsense - did it bite you?'

'No, it threatened to, it struck at me and showed me its fangs, but I told it that if it bit me or bit Patience I would have it for my supper.'

Flame looked at me as if for the first time then suddenly howled with laughter. He did what I can only describe as a performance of what he thought a fierce hedgehog might look like, arching his back to try and make it look spiny and tip-toeing around while snarling; and then he laughed again even louder, rolling on his back and scaring a flock of little birds who had been gathering in a nearby bush.

'You... you told...' he struggled to control his giggling, '...I'd better watch myself or you'll be eating ME next!' He paused to look at me and it seemed to amuse him, his intelligent eyes twinkled with mirth, 'Well... blow my brush right off and bite my bum!' he exclaimed, '...Even humans are scared of adders and now you - a hedgehog, a small hedgehog, a small WHITE hedgehog, threatened to eat one for his supper. Ohhh, Mother was right; you CAN learn something from every creature. What a brave little prickly white thing you are!'

'I certainly didn't feel very brave at the time,' I said.

'I'll bet you didn't,' Flame nodded in agreement, 'I would have been a little nervous if I were to meet an adder - and I'm the bravest creature in the Great Outside - apart from you of course.'

It was nice that Flame seemed to like me. We drank together at the river and afterwards he dug rapidly and furiously at the loose soil on the edge of the field which unearthed several fat worms, providing me with the best meal in a long time. Then, explaining it was time once again to pursue the mysterious female fox; he said his goodbyes and bounded off into the darkening woods.

There followed a long and exhausting walk home. Dawn had left when I finally arrived and so I curled up and thought of many things. The fear of meeting Flame had now gone; in fact it would be nice if we met again soon, he was good company.

I thought of Patience and hoped she had enjoyed a safe and successful day's hunting. I also thought of Rain and Puddle, my brothers; I had not scented them today, maybe they had gone further away to find their own territories as hedgehogs mostly do.

Finally, I thought of what to do next.

Leaving this home and making my own somewhere else might be a big risk being - as Mother had said - a rather special little hedgehog; it would probably be more sensible to stay for a while and wait to see what my sister Dawn was going to do.

It rained heavily all the next day. The noise was a constant drumming outside the entrance and little rivers trickled down the hill to the field carrying grubs and tiny snails flooded out of their homes.

I had eaten so well, thanks to Flame, that I was able to remain at home where it was dry, occasionally popping my head out to catch some water that dripped off the overhanging bush.

It rained all through the night too and it was not until the following afternoon that it eased off so that, to my relief, it was possible to leave home and get out once more. The air was sweet and fresh after the storm and the ground was muddy and soft.

All kinds of insects sang in celebration of seeing the sun again and the Great Outside looked so inviting, just waiting to be explored.

I doubt the relief of leaving my home would have felt so good if I had known it was the last time I would ever see it.

* * *

9

Moon-Eyed Beasts

Food. All creatures need it. It's the most important thing there is, along with water. So, if I talk a lot about going out, looking for food, finding a meal and then returning home well-fed and relieved, it's because, for hedgehogs, that is a great day - a victory.

We never know when we set out hunting whether we will find food or whether something bigger - and also out looking for food - will find us! All wild creatures (and many humans) live this way.

So, on a chilly evening when big spots of rain were being blown around by a gusty wind it was necessary to set out alone to find food and drink.

It is difficult to hear in the wind and scents are also much harder to pinpoint; there is a danger the worrying scent you think you are walking away from may be right up ahead of you. It is a time to be especially alert.

Because of the amount of rain that had fallen I felt sure Mother's Pool would provide a drink without me having to walk all the way down to the river. And so it did, it was full to overflowing while from across the wide field the excitable and playful wind carried the scent of a Flame Beast from the human nest.

It was getting colder in both the days and nights and, as Mother had taught us, the daylights were getting shorter and the nights longer.

Those who, like me, had never seen a winter before wondered just how long it would be before it came and blanketed the Great Outside in white.

I drank at Mother's Pool and then paused to scent the air before deciding where to hunt. Skirting the edge of the field away from the direction of the woods, I headed for the far side of what we now called Hedgehog Hill, the place of home. Long grass and bushes were there and maybe some late berries still hung from the lowest brambles.

A day like any other then; hedgehogs don't get bored, every hunt is an adventure, we cannot afford to daydream when we must continually scent the air and keep eyes and ears open.

I was just wondering if anyone I knew was around when on the wind came a familiar scent, very faint but unmistakable - and there was something worryingly wrong with it. The direction it was coming from made me more and more worried; even allowing for the trickery of the wind.

Hedgehogs, and many other creatures, can read the news with their noses. We know who is in the area, whether they are happy, worried, curious or sad and this scent told me that my friend, Patience the mouse, was very, very frightened

Patience, of course, is often frightened; she fears most things; she's a mouse and has reason to be nervous. But this was different. With Flame the Fox and Sunn the Adder she had been afraid of what was possibly going to happen. This scent told me that something had already happened - and it was something terrible!

Patience had been close to this spot recently and then met with disaster. Now there was a trail of this disturbing scent leading out into the wide field. She was my friend and there was no way this could simply be ignored.

Also, if there was something new and dangerous in the area it paid to learn about it; so I left the comfort of the long grass of my little hill and headed out into the unknown.

This field was once covered with very high grass, the shade of the morning sun. It was put there by humans who then came and cut it all down again. Now there was little growing and so not a lot of cover for a white hedgehog. It was a relief when the trail led me closer to the edge of the field.

The trail now began heading directly toward the line of bushes which separates the field from the path of the Moon-Eyed Beasts. This was far beyond the boundaries of my family's hunting grounds and unfamiliar territory. Such a journey went against all my instincts, but Patience had given me a gift of knowledge and so helping her in return was a wise and kind thing to do.

Under a cloudy sky, evening turned into a gloomy half-light and finally into darkness. There was now quite a distance between me and my home and it was doubtful a way back could be found before dawn. The only direction then was forward, following the trail of the scent Patience had left behind. There was another scent accompanying it now, a disturbing one that worried me even more.

The scent was getting stronger and the distance covered had gone unnoticed while concentrating on the trail Patience had left.

The clouds were breaking up and in the light of an almost full moon a tall straight line of bushes loomed right in front of me - and the trail of the scent led through them and beyond.

Going into the bushes was easy, there was a path which appeared to be well-used by many creatures and contained many scents, most of which I did not recognise but among them were the increasingly strong scent of Patience and whatever was travelling with her.

Resting for a short while in the safety of the bushes, a distant noise alerted me to a new threat. It was a noise I had frequently heard from far away across the fields but now, close-up, it was the loudest noise ever and it hurt my ears.

A Moon-Eyed Beast was coming!

The ground shuddered beneath my feet and then the beast's eyes glowed through the branches like twin moons only much, much brighter.

As it passed it seemed as if the whole world became as light as day and the roar was terrifying, then it rushed away followed by a pair of bright red twinkles and the scent of a Flame Beast. I waited a long time before daring to venture out to cross the wide path.

The surface of the path was hard and cold, there was no way anything could scratch for food in it. Although narrow, looking from side to side it appeared to go on forever, a completely flat dark ribbon in the moonlight. The other side beckoned but when only halfway across the worst happened and, with a tremble, I realised another Moon-Eyed Beast was approaching.

Flame the Fox can flash across a field at full stretch and birds streak across the sky so quickly it is hard for my eyes to follow them, but a Moon-Eyed Beast is faster than everything. And it roars all the time without stopping to breathe! It sounded angry as if in pursuit of something even faster. There was no chance of reaching safety before the creature got to me.

Its eyes got larger and brighter and it roared as if all the creatures of the Great Outside were squealing at once. And it was so, so big.

As it drew close its twin eyes towered high above and either side of me its feet tore along the path without ever leaving it.

The moonlit clouds disappeared and were replaced by the creature's belly and then, in a blink, it was over and racing into the distance. For a moment fear froze me to the hard path but then I scurried as fast as possible to reach the other side with my heart racing.

I could so easily have been trampled under its feet; it could not have seen me. But now, on the other side of the path, the presence of Patience was stronger and fresher. And passing through another line of bushes found me in a sort of small field where the grass was very short and the scent of strange creatures mingled with that of my friend.

Looking around in the light of the moon the large bulk of the human stone nest loomed close by but the scent led me away from it, to a smaller human nest made from strangely-shaped wood. There was a trail leading around this odd building to where a scent told me my friend was very close. So close that on turning a corner I expected to see her.

But it was no mouse waiting to greet me.

The creature studying me was much larger than a mouse - much larger than me too, with big, front-facing eyes like those of a fox - but this was no fox. It moved silently toward me, sitting just a pace or two away, licking its lips, its tongue passing over a set of sharp-looking teeth.

'Looking for someone?' it asked; its voice was warm and smooth, like Mother's used to be, but where hers was full of kindness, there was a chilling air of menace about this creature. 'Errr, yes – I'm seeking my friend,' I replied nervously.

It reached out a foot toward me and I noticed with surprise that as the foot approached a set of claws, curved and cruel-looking, sprang from its paw. The claws brushed against my back and jerked away quickly; the creature gave off a loud hiss.

'Thought so, you're a hedgehog - strange colour but a hedgehog still - and just as painful,' the creature's voice was hypnotic. 'Your friend... mouse?'

'Y... Yes,' I replied already fearing the worst.

'My apologies...' the creature said, '...but a cat's got to eat.'

*   *   *

10

I am Called Zephyr

I felt like crying for the first time since losing Mother.

'She was called Patience,' I said; the cat seemed unimpressed by this information, '...and she had lived through a winter!'

'Well if she stays hidden under this shed she might well live through another one - crafty little squeak!'

I must have looked confused because the cat turned to me and sighed, 'Yes, that's right, it got away - played dead as I carried it all the way here - and then when I put it down it suddenly sprang to life and shot under the floor of the shed; and now I can't get to the blasted thing. Really annoying - an elementary mistake, my mother would have been ashamed of me.'

Patience was alive. I felt like squealing with joy, forgetting for a moment my present position. This was one of the creatures Mother had told us lived with humans, a cat.

Cats were hunters and killers, they were very clever and they solved problems - but they could also be cruel - and this cat had just been tricked out of a meal by a mouse and would not be in a very good mood. Would an introduction help?

'My name is Northwind,' I said politely.

The cat studied me coldly.

'I'm not in the least bit surprised,' it replied, 'I am called Zephyr, which is a wind that blows from the west, so we have something in common. That's my real name by the way - the name my Mother gave me; the humans have another name for me, which I can't possibly pronounce of course, but whenever they make that noise I know it's me they are referring to.'

The cat stood, paced around the edge of what he had called a 'shed' and then returned.

'That mouse isn't going to come out any time soon, is it?'

'She will be terrified,' I said, 'Please leave her alone.'

'I suppose I could...' Zephyr looked at me in a disturbing way, '...I suppose I could eat you instead.'

Suddenly very frightened, I instinctively curled into a ball for protection.

Zephyr chuckled, 'Oh good, I do like games,' he said smoothly. 'You curl into a ball and I will sit next to you; let's see who goes to sleep and relaxes first. I will only need you to drop your guard for the shortest of times. In fact, the only things that strike quicker than me are adders and lightning.'

'I survived a meeting with an adder,' I mumbled from within my ball.

'Really? Well, that's adders for you, they can go an age without eating - me on the other hand, oh, I'm always hungry.

The humans feed me of course but nothing quite takes the place of a successful hunt. It always tastes better when you do-it-yourself I find.'

Remaining curled into a ball for very long was not going to be easy, it had been an exhausting journey to get here and as Zephyr had explained, it only took a moment off guard for him to attack.

'Can't we just be friends?' I asked.

'Of course,' Zephyr purred, 'Some of my best ever meals were friends, the friendliest thing you could do would be to let me eat you. Look, I really don't want to wait out here all night and I promise you, the end is going to be the same so why drag this out?'

The cat stood, stretched, then came closer and sat right next to me. 'You don't look like any hedgehog I've ever seen - do you think you taste the same?'

Recalling something Flame had said on our first meeting gave me an idea, 'I am probably poisonous,' I said.

Zephyr chuckled, 'Hmmm, possible I suppose, but then, if you were poisonous, you wouldn't need the prickles, would you? You'd have some... warning colours or something. No, you're not poisonous - and you're getting tired, I can tell; sleepy... sleeeeepy, such a long walk and your eyelids are soooo heavy... just close them for a few moments... sleeeeepy.'

There was little doubt I would lose concentration before this cat did, even though I was so scared. I could scent Patience hidden under the boards of the shed floor; and then I heard her, she was moving.

I could see Zephyr's ears prick up and he turned to look toward the shed, he had heard it too. A small and familiar whiskered face peered out.

'Cat - here cat, leave him alone, he be only young.'

Zephyr stood, smiling his curious smile; he blinked in the light of the moon as he studied the emerging mouse.

'If you must eat me then you must, I doubt I would see it through another winter anyway; but please, let Northwind go!'

Zephyr's mock compassion failed to hide his cruel glee, 'Awww, how nice it must be for both of you to have such a good friend; all I've got is a dog and he's not much fun; sleeps, eats and wees, never washes - smelly, boring old fleabag. There are the humans of course but I don't understand them, they mean well but... ah that's humans for you.'

Zephyr turned away from me and padded silently toward Patience who was trembling, but not running away. It was the bravest thing I had ever seen.

'Fair enough,' Zephyr said breezily, 'I'll make do with a mouse and you can scurry back to your field, I wasn't looking forward to pricked paws anyway. I hope you appreciate this, White-Hog; loyalty is a rare and special thing, always remember - you had one true friend.'

Zephyr turned his attention to Patience and crouched, wiggling his bottom as if to pounce. I was too shocked and heartbroken to speak, but a voice came from behind me that shocked me even more.

'He's got more than one friend, actually.'

Zephyr spun around, eyes wide with shock; looking behind me he hissed, showing a vicious set of teeth, his back arched and his fur fluffed up until he looked twice his size. He growled deeply and started backing away. The voice spoke again.

'Seeing as you enjoy games, here's one you might like, it's called, "Let's see if a cat fits inside a fox" - ready?'

I turned to see Flame showing the cat a fine set of teeth.

'Flame!' I cried with relief.

With a final loud hiss and a deep growl Zephyr shot off into the flower beds that grew to the side of the shed. Patience forgot her natural fear of foxes and scurried out to greet us.

'Oh... I really thought that was the end of me... oh... Northwind... Flame... thank you, thank you,' she gasped, speaking so fast the words fell into one another.

Flame shook his head and turned to me, 'Squeaky snack - told you she'd be trouble, didn't I? Lucky, I happened to be passing and scented the pair of you.'

I had never been more pleased to see Flame, 'Well I'm so glad you're here - what a brave and clever fox you are.'

Flame grinned, 'Of course, told you, didn't I? You won't find a braver or a cleverer fox in all the Great Outside. Now then, this is a bit too close to humans for my liking; I suggest you and twitchy whiskers start heading homewards.'

Then it suddenly got light. Not by the sun coming up - which makes it get light slowly; this happened suddenly. The whole of where we were became light. The sun was not due to rise for a long, long time but, from nowhere, a different sun - similar to the bright eyes of a Moon-Eyed Beast, flooded everything with light and a voice like I had never heard before.

'Falstaff, come on! Puss, Puss, Puss...'

'Oh no - humans,' Flame's ears pricked up, 'Not good, I'd hide if I were you.'

Patience panicked, 'I've never been this far away before and I don't know the way home.'

Flame sighed, 'I can't believe I'm about to say this but - do you want a lift?'

'A lift,' Patience sounded confused.

'I'll carry you.' Flame said urgently, 'But hurry up and decide because I'm probably not welcome around here.'

'You are suggesting I climb into a fox's mouth?' Patience looked horrified.

'Yes - or you can stay here and renew your friendship with Zephyr; look, I know your name, I won't eat you - I promise.'

'Go on Patience, you can trust Flame and I'll be fine, I'll see you back home.' I urged.

'Very well, please don't bite too hard,' Patience screwed-up her eyes and Flame stooped, taking her gently in his mouth.

From the human nest the voice called out again, this time accompanied by a harsh barking which clearly alarmed Flame. He put Patience down and growled fearfully, 'Dog - do that rollie-up thing you creatures do Northwind.'

'What's a dog?' I asked as the barking and human voice drew closer.

'A bit like me only not so handsome - see you back home Frosty Face!' He picked Patience up again and was gone in a flash through the hedge.

A creature came bounding out of the light toward me; I curled into a ball again. This was no cat, it sniffed at me in the same way Flame had when we first met. It was similar in shape to Flame but more heavily built. It stopped next to me and repeated its shouting which hurt my ears at such short range.

'I'm on guard! ...I'm on guard!' it shouted.

Then another voice called from out of the light - the human voice.

The creature, a 'Dog' Flame had called it, turned in response to the human voice and shouted once more. Then something approached which was so different to everything I had ever seen that it might not even have been another creature.

So tall, its head seemed far away, high up. And it walked on just two... legs, very long legs. Its front legs never seemed to touch the ground and it carried a sun, like the big sun that had suddenly lit everything but this one was smaller. It appeared to have seen me and let out a cry that could have meant anything.

Both Mother and Flame had told me humans did not usually hurt hedgehogs and so, despite the size of the creature, there was less fear than there had been when facing Zephyr. Then its legs folded and the creature's head came down, lower and lower, getting bigger and bigger as I unfolded and squinted up at it.

Its eyes were huge; there was no hair or fur on its face but long hair surrounding it. Its body was covered in a strangeness that was neither fur nor hair. It looked away and called out then returned its attention to me. It made more noises, quieter ones as if it was trying to communicate but the sounds made no sense at all.

Then it did another very strange thing. It seemed to take off part of its skin and wrap it around the ends of its front legs. It then lowered these legs down to me and, without hurting me, wrapped me in its hold and raised me up.

I rose up and up until I was level with the creature's face and those huge eyes. It made more soft noises. There followed the unbelievable strangeness of seeing things from above for the very first time and the fear of looking down. Then the creature turned around, still holding me, and moved quickly towards its nest.

And my life changed forever.

*　　*　　*

This diary belongs to: Lillie Marsh

<u>October 1st</u>

Rain in the night.

    I have been a teenager now for 24 days but Mum and Dad are still treating me like a twelve-year-old!

    I wanted to go home for tea with Rosie after school and then into town with her and her Mum to an auction which would have been cool! But Mum said we had to go home because we are off to see Gran and Granddad tomorrow and it's a long drive.

    It wouldn't have been a long drive if we hadn't moved from the City all the way out here to the middle of nowhere...

...Where nothing exciting happens and I have less friends than anyone – anywhere – EVER!

AND I'm going to miss school tomorrow, a Friday, which is the day I really enjoy because we have music and art and biology – which I will certainly need when I become a vet!!

I have tried to practice bandaging on Toby but he just rolls over for me to tickle his tummy and Falstaff is always out somewhere chasing birds or squirrels. I wish he wasn't such a bully.

Not looking forward to tomorrow, I hate long journeys and even though I want to be in the City again!

I know it is going to make me miserable because I won't be able to stay there and see all my friends.

They are all having great lives, going to events and the cinema and parties. There is so much to see and do there and all there is here are fields and hedges and more fields and woods and mud and cow's poo.

I may as well go to bed. There is nothing on TV and none of my friends are online – they are all probably out having fun.

I can hear an owl, actually it's two owls, people don't know that. If you hear a too-whit too-whoo it's two owls talking to each other, never a single owl. I wonder what they are talking about?

Goodnight diary xxx

October 3rd - Morning

Cold but bright and sunny.

Well I was right; it was a long and boring drive and when we got to the city all my friends were in school – it being a Friday and so I couldn't catch up with anyone. I messaged a few of my friends but they are not allowed to use their phones in class. They texted back when we were on our way home but it was too late then!

It was nice to see Gran and Granddad though. They gave me a voucher to download some music and some money for clothes which was very kind of them.

It is Saturday today, I am going to ask Mum if she will give me a lift into town so I can meet up with Rosie and go shopping.

There is only one clothes shop in town and they don't sell any cool clothes so I will probably save my clothes money until I go to the city again – but I don't know when that will be.

Afternoon:

It was a nice day in town. The cafe was closed but there is a small cafe in the antique shop and so Rosie and I had cake and a drink in there.

We saw a lady with a ~~Pyrane~~ ~~Pyrren~~ Pyrenean Mountain Dog (I had to look the spelling up).
It was HUGE, the dog was called Brock. I took a picture of him.
I stayed at Rosie's for tea and then Dad picked me up.

<u>Evening:</u>

<u>*** STOP PRESS!! ***</u>

What is the most AMAZING creature you have ever seen? Not in zoos or on TV but <u>REALLY</u>? In real life?

We had drawn the curtains. Mum and Dad were watching TV while I was on my tablet talking to Gemma, one of my friends in the city. We heard a howling from the garden. It sounded like Falstaff being really annoyed with something.

We have had visits from a fox recently who we think is interested in our chickens. It will not come too close though because it can smell Toby and foxes are usually scared of dogs.

Dad looked out but could see nothing and so I took a torch and went outside.

When the security light came on we saw it was a fox which ran away quickly when Toby rushed out barking. I walked down the garden to look for Falstaff, who I found on top of the shed with his tail all fluffed up as if he had had a big shock.

Toby was still barking as if he was trying to show me something. He had spotted a creature in the grass of the lawn. I went to calm him down and then I saw... IT!

I looked at it for a long time because I had never seen anything like it before in my whole life. It looked a bit scary but it was clearly far more frightened of me.

It was a hedgehog!!!

I know that sounds ordinary but imagine a hedgehog's ghost! That's what this creature looked like. It was a hedgehog – but pure white with pink eyes. I took my cardigan off and wrapped it around my hands, I knelt down and picked it up; it curled itself into a ball.

I couldn't see very clearly in the dark of the garden and so I carried it back into the house. Falstaff got down off the shed and followed us in. Toby still seemed excited by what I was carrying but at least he had stopped barking.

Inside the house I called to Mum and Dad who were amazed at the little creature. Dad said it was an albino hedgehog and a male one and that they are probably very rare.

He said I should just let it go in the garden but I was afraid that the fox or Falstaff would hurt it so I persuaded Dad to make a little nest out of an old crate in the wood shed and we would keep it until the next night and then let it go.

I checked online later and found that only one in 10,000 hedgehogs are albinos so I am very, very lucky to have discovered one.

We put it in the box with some dry leaves from under the wood shed and gave it a bit of dog food and some water but it didn't seem very hungry. It was still frightened I think.

I am going to go online and learn as much as I can about hedgehogs – especially ghost ones! So that I will know what is best to do...

...I have just been in the wood shed and checked him, he seems to be sleeping and I think he has eaten a little bit of food.

What an amazing day.

My first patient – and I am going to take good care of him!

I am going to call him *<u>JACK</u>* because he makes me think of Jack Frost!

Goodnight diary

(And goodnight Jack ♥)

Lillie xxx

*   *   *

11

Into The Human Nest

I was travelling high above the land - not as high as the birds, but much higher than any hedgehog is meant to be!

We are ground creatures and know the soil of the fields and hedgerows and the living things of the forest floor. We know the tastes and scents of the different leaves that have fallen, the twigs and nuts, and the safe, safe surroundings of the earth and our underground homes.

Now that all seemed far away and nothing here made me feel secure - and yet there seemed to be no real danger. The tall creature carried me into the human nest which turned out to be a very strange place.

Outside it was night, but inside this vast home it was as light as day, even lighter in fact, with no clouds to hide their sun, and it was as warm as summer. All kinds of strange shaped things were in there as well as more humans, two - both of them even bigger, it seemed, than the human who had carried me in.

Their faces came close to me and they made lots of their strange human noises. I was then carried from that place through other big spaces and to the outside again. It came as a relief to see the sky and the clouds passing across the moon.

But it was still too high for comfort as we passed into another, smaller, human nest. This one smelled of the woods and trees. I thought at first I was falling and was frightened but then I realised the human holding me was slowly lowering me to the ground. It put me in a thing with a floor and walls about the size of a hedgehog home. Inside was a pile of dry leaves.

This home had a hole in the side big enough for me to get out if needed but I was too frightened to move much. Then two small round human things were lowered and put on the floor next to the box, Curiosity made me take a look which made the humans' chatter even louder.

One of the round things had a puddle in it and the other contained something unfamiliar but smelled like it might be food. I withdrew my nose back into the home and was surprised when one of the humans lowered a roof on to it which made it dark and a much more natural place.

The leaves in the home contained many scents. Mice had passed over them at some time, many insects and even a snake - but not an adder. There was nothing in the scents to make me fearful and so the task began to make myself a little nest. I was so, so tired, but hungry too.

The humans had gone and there was no sound but for some distant mice, unknown bird noises far away and a wind that had picked up and was now shaking and rattling this odd place.

Checking the surroundings brought no sign of danger so it was time to try a little of what promised to be food. It tasted nice but there is always a risk in the unknown. Even though this home was put there by humans and was not a natural home, it was probably the safest place to be in these surroundings and so I returned to my nest of leaves and closed my eyes.

What a strange day it had been - and what wonderful friends Patience and Flame were. I wondered when I would see them again.

I awoke in daylight and saw my new surroundings properly for the first time. This was a large human nest full of great piles of wood which had been somehow broken into smaller pieces and placed on top of each other to make hills.

The food and puddle were still there inviting me to eat and drink. It was strange being able to do this without having to walk and hunt for it. There were no other signs of life although the air was full of odd scents. It was time to explore.

Hedgehogs are curious about their surroundings and always eager to learn new things. There were mice living in one of the great hills of wood and so I called out to them.

'Hello - mice... hello - are you home?'

There was no answer, so they may have been asleep or so shocked by hearing a hedgehog they had decided to hide.

I was about to explore behind one of the hills when a huge opening appeared in the far wall through which it was possible see the Great Outside. A human entered, it appeared to be the one from the previous night who had carried me through the human nest; it moved quickly on its long back legs toward the home it had put there for me; removing the roof it lowered itself to look in.

It rose up to its full height again and began looking around. It had probably expected to find me in the small home and was now wondering where I was.

It crossed my mind to scurry behind one of the wooden hills, but it would only be a matter of time before discovery - also there was the possibility the hill might fall on me; so I remained still, knowing the human would soon see me. I was unafraid; if these creatures had meant to eat me they would surely have done so by now.

Sure enough, the human spotted me easily enough, a little white hedgehog on the dark wooden ground. Making human noises the creature lowered itself and gently picked me up, all the way up, to get a good look at me with those huge eyes.

Humans, we had been taught, can make really loud noises when they are excited, but it seemed this human was being quiet on purpose so as not to frighten me. It made soft noises like the wind, the same as hedgehogs do when they are talking and something possibly dangerous is close by.

I decided to call this human 'Whisper;' it seemed a friendly creature.

Whisper lowered me into the home and lifted the things with food and a puddle in them, then left; and almost straight away returned with a fresh puddle and some more food. Humans certainly seemed to know what hedgehogs liked and this one made more soothing noises as I gratefully enjoyed an easy meal.

The other two humans also visited and seemed interested in me. Could this have been because, as Mother used to say, I was a special little hedgehog? The scent of Zephyr hung in the air just outside the human nest, also that of the dog who had shouted at me on our first meeting, but they did not enter.

Much of that day was spent in sleep thanks to being well fed and fully rested after my adventures. It was dark when I next woke and there was a familiar foxy voice whispering harshly from just outside the human nest.

'Northwind - hey... Northwind - I know you're in there, I can scent you - are you alright?'

It was great to hear my friend and to know he was here.

'Flame - I'm in here, I'm fine, the humans have fed me and given me a place to rest.'

I scurried out of my home and headed for the wall of the human nest. There was a small gap where the wall did not quite reach the floor and I laughed as Flame's nose pushed under it.

'Did you get Patience home safely?' I asked.

'Her? Oh yes, I had to put her down twice, her whiskers were tickling me. I warned her, if she made me sneeze she was walking the rest of the way. Can you get out of that shed?'

'I don't know' I replied, 'It's a strange place.'

'Yes, you're in a wood shed, it's where the humans keep the wood they feed a Flame Beast with. There's one living in their main nest and if you don't keep feeding them, they die. They die if they get wet too.'

'I'm not sure if I can get out,' I replied, 'I have slept most of the time and I haven't explored properly yet.'

'Ha ha - dozy hedgehog!' Flame laughed. 'By the way, the human that picked you up is a young female; it gave me some human food last winter, so I think you can trust it.'

There was a sudden barking from the direction of the human nest.

'Oh, it's that wobbling windbag of a dog again! I'm off, I'll be back later.'

I heard Flame rush off, but it was cheering to know my friend knew where I was and that Patience was home safe and sound.

But was there a way out of here?

*   *   *

October 4th – Chilly morning.

It had been a cold night and I was worried that Jack was OK. But the wood shed is usually warm and Dad said he is going to put a heater in there to make sure my patient is comfortable.

I checked him this morning, he is beautiful, when I picked him up he made really cute little grunts and squeaks as if he was trying to talk. He didn't seem nervous.

I spoke to him but I'm not sure he understood in the way cats and dogs can understand.

It would be nice to keep him but he is a wild animal and needs to live free. There is a hole in the wall at the rear of the woodshed big enough for him to get out of. I have made sure there is a path to it through the logs. If he wants to leave he can – but I hope he stays.

I can't wait to show him to Rosie. I puta picture of him on my timeline and he's already got 37 likes!

I've got homework to do but I really don't want to do it. It's all about weather patterns and not very interesting. Liam Connor cut and pasted an essay about the Murray-Darling River and was told off for cheating.

He had to write another essay about why ~~plague~~ plagiarism is wrong.

 It is a nice day and I can smell Sunday lunch cooking. Sundays can be a bit boring with no one to talk to and nowhere to go. Dad has to go away to work again for a few days next week, I miss him when he's gone but Mum and I are going to go into town tomorrow evening so I might meet up with Rosie. I wish I could take Jack but I think a trip in the car would really freak him out.

 Sunday lunch... HOORAY!!!
 Lillie xxx

 *   *   *

12

What Do You Think Humans Eat?

My deep sleep was disturbed by the sound of Whisper approaching. She lifted the roof off the home; I wish she wouldn't do that. Homes are meant to have roofs which should never come off; but of course, this was a home made by humans, not hedgehogs and they probably don't know how to build a proper one.

She picked me up, which I'm getting used to but I'm not very fond of. It's frightening and not a natural thing for hedgehogs. Perhaps she just likes looking at me or is curious. Would it be difficult to make her understand?

'My name is Northwind, please don't keep picking me up and please don't take the roof off my home, it's a bit disturbing when that happens.'

Mother had told us once that badgers could sometimes dig the roofs off hedgehog homes to get at them and even though I'm pretty sure Whisper does not want to hurt me, especially after Flame had told me of her kindness to him, it still makes me nervous.

She clearly didn't understand me at all. She made some human noises then lowered me back into the home and replaced the roof but now, fully awake, it was time to explore.

There was something to eat and a fresh puddle outside, Whisper had retreated to the far side of the wood shed and the food and drink was most welcome.

Humans do curious things that no other creature appears to do. Whisper seemed to be trying to hide her face behind a small dark object, she would hold it close to me; it smelled of alien human things and there was nothing of the Great Outside about it. She made more human noises; it is clearly their attempt at speech.

After eating, the presence of Whisper made exploring uncomfortable; it felt better to retreat once more into this human-built home. Then she left and so I ventured out again planning to have a good look around.

It takes a little time to become used to the size of human buildings. At first, they seem huge but really, they are tiny compared to the Great Outside and it was possible to walk all around this 'wood shed' in a short time. And there was the discovery, as suspected, that I was not alone.

'Are you a hedgehog?'

The voice came from above me somewhere high up in the hills of broken wood. A pair of mice looked down curiously.

'Yes, I'm a hedgehog, but I'm white; my name is Northwind,' I answered politely. 'Do you live here?'

'Indeed,' the mouse replied, 'We came in here to hide from the cat when summer had just begun but it seemed safe and warm and we can get in and out for food so we've stayed, there's a whole family of us here now. My name is Watcher and this is my sister, Silence.'

'I'm very pleased to meet you,' I said.

'We can show you a way to get out,' Watcher said, 'It's behind one of these piles of wood right in the corner of the shed. It should be just big enough for a hedgehog to squeeze through but, be careful - a fox is often sniffing around here at night.'

'Yes, he's a friend of mine,' I told them and they stood up on their back legs in shock!

They led me through a pile of wood to the corner of the shed where there was indeed a hole just about big enough for a hedgehog to get through. It almost made me squeal with happiness to know escape into the Great Outside was possible. I could now make my way home.

But this would require a lot of thought.

There was still much to learn and, really, there did not appear to be any danger here although it was very, very strange. The food was regular and good, water was close by and nothing that was likely to eat me could get into the little home the humans had made for me.

And there was one more thing; something very big was coming, everything could feel it, especially in the mornings and the middle of the night.

The trees knew it and were shedding their leaves, closing down and preparing for sleep; the birds knew it and were flying away; the bats and mice knew it was coming and were preparing for the long night.

The hedgehogs felt it too of course - and even the humans felt it and they fed their Flame Beast more and more, fearing the killing cold that was heading here as winter got ready to sweep over the Great Outside, turning everything white.

It was still almost as warm as summer in the shed and there were clearly a lot worse places to spend the winter. It was to be my first cold season and there was so much unknown about what was to come. Patience had lived through a winter and had told of how hard the ground became, making it difficult to forage for food.

Flame had also seen the last winter and had told me just how tough it could be to survive when even the water turned so hard nothing could drink it. How could any creature live like that?

Flame was of course (as he so often reminded me) a very clever fox. He could catch rabbits and other small creatures and he had a thick, warm coat.

But how would a small white hedgehog survive in such a cruel and cold time? Of course, my sister and brothers were out there somewhere, probably getting ready for the long night. They would know what to do to keep warm. They would have been eating as much as possible so that they were big enough to survive for such a long time without food.

But was I big enough? Would my home in the side of the little hill remain warm enough for me? So, after a lot of thinking, I decided it might be wise to stay here in this shed for my first winter and hope the humans would keep bringing food and puddles. Then, when the Great Outside came back to life it would be time to head off back to my old home and do the things hedgehogs are supposed to do.

Now that I knew there was a way out of the shed, however, it would be possible to meet up with Flame when he came to visit. I couldn't wait to see him and to tell him my plan.

'Are you mad?' Flame looked at me in amazement.

A cold moon shone down on the patch of longer grass behind the wood shed close to a few small fruit trees. Having squeezed through the hole in the corner of the shed on hearing Flame sniffing around and calling out for me in a low voice, I was now nibbling on a fallen apple while Flame sat nearby, eyes and ears on the alert for the dog or any nosey humans.

The fox studied me, head on one side as if trying to make sense of my plan. His intelligent eyes flickered in the bright moonlight, full of curiosity and mischief.

'You are actually planning to stay here, in this... this human building for the winter?'

'I thought it was a good plan - you told me the Great Outside was a dangerous place when the cold comes.' I said.

Flame sniffed at an apple and took a small bite; he wrinkled his nose but still attempted to eat the rest of the fruit.

'It is - but... listen Northwind, what do you think humans eat?'

Strangely, it had never occurred to me. Obviously, they must eat something and, being big, quite a lot of whatever it was - but, surely not hedgehogs?

'Not... hedgehogs?' I asked nervously.

'Probably,' said Flame, '...they are living things like us - they'll eat anything; and in the winter when there's not much food around they'll probably eat you. They store wood to feed their Flame Beasts, how do you know what they're storing you for?'

What Flame said made sense - and he was a very clever fox - but, how could one tiny thing like me possibly feed a human? If they were storing hedgehogs for food, there would surely be lots of them. However, there was no denying they were strange and there was much about their lives no creature understood.

Flame put his head close to mine and whispered harshly, 'What do you think the chickens are for?'

'Chickens?' I must have sounded puzzled. Flame shook his head, 'So much to learn,' he muttered; 'yes, chickens... bwaaak cluck cluck cluck?'

I laughed, 'Yes, I've heard that, lots of them I think, and quite nearby. They sound a bit... birdy.'

'Yes, well they sound a bit birdy because they ARE a bit birdy, except they can't fly so you don't get all those weird sky words that most birds use. Round, feathery things they are - taste a bit like duck according to my father. Why do you think they're here, with the humans?'

'I see what you mean,' I responded, '...but if they liked eating hedgehogs wouldn't there be lots of them in the woodshed?'

Flame looked thoughtful. 'Good point, I've never seen humans hunting hedgehogs but then the fools hunt things they have no intention of eating! There's no telling with them.'

He paused to crunch a piece of apple and swallow it, the bitterness caused him to screw up his face in disgust, 'Horrible,' he croaked; and then he turned to me, 'Come with me, come on.'

He trotted off slowly with me scurrying to keep up. We passed around the side of the wood shed and across the corner of a much bigger area of short grass. Behind I could now make out the 'inside sunlight' from the human nest.

'Come on, hurry up, I don't want to be caught out here - and neither do you; but you must see this.'

Taking a deep breath, I hurried on after my friend.

*   *   *

13

Are You a Pet?

Flame led the way by the light of the moon and we headed for the dark shadows beneath the trees where the short grass turns into the wilderness we know best.

Moving on between two thick bushes we crossed an area of small stones which the fox passed over with ease but which slowed me down, causing my friend to hurry me up.

'I'm doing my best' I whispered, 'My legs are not as long as yours!'

Finally, we were in a place behind the human nest where some very strange looking things stood. They were large, almost as large as the wood shed but not as tall, and they smelled of old heat and Flame Beast and strange sharp odours I had encountered only once before.

'See those things...' Flame indicated the strange objects, 'Do you know what they are?'

It took a little bit of thinking but then, suddenly, I remembered those scents and the terrifying experience that came with them.

'They're... they're Moon-Eyed Beasts!' I said in awe. 'Are they sleeping?'

'Is that what you call them? Good name; foxes call them "Carriers," they carry humans and other things over great distances very quickly,' Flame explained. 'But they cannot see or hear on their own and they cannot move without humans inside them. Foxes believe they are not really alive at all, they are just things that humans use, like we might use a log to float across a river.'

'They seem alive at night,' I shuddered, 'One of them went right over the top of me.'

Flame looked at me sideways, his eyes full of humour; 'Adders... Moon-Eyed Beasts... humans... cats... Do you know, I think you're the luckiest hedgehog alive! In fact, I'll bet if a badger tried to eat you, all its teeth would drop out or something.'

Flame always made me laugh; it was true, I had indeed been a very lucky little hedgehog so far and meeting a friend like Flame was probably the luckiest thing of all.

'Right, listen Northwind,' he said, 'Come to this spot - in the day would be best - and if you see that both of these Carriers - or Moon-Eyed Beasts or whatever you want to call them, are missing; then it means the humans are not around - and when that happens there's something I think you should do...'

*　　*　　*

<u>October 11th - Really chilly, but sunny.</u>

I have not written in my diary for a week because I have been so busy with school work and helping Mum make a costume for the play she is in. She is playing the part of a woman who gets shipwrecked and pretends to be her brother or something. William Shakespeare wrote it.

Jack is fit and well, I think he might have decided to stay with us. He seems bigger, it must be the good food and rest he is having. Dad has made him a proper hedgehog house now, he downloaded the plan and it is in the woodshed where it is warm.

There is a small heater in there to keep the logs dry and it means Jack will not freeze in the winter. The lid comes off to clean it out but I don't lift the roof off very much now when Jack is in there as I don't think he likes it.

Someone from our local paper, The Bugle, read one of my posts about Jack and they want to send a reporter and photographer here to write a story about him and take a picture – he's going to be a celebrity! He might even end up on the TV!

Rosie's Auntie's dog was on TV once for winning a prize.

I don't think Toby would win a prize –
unless there is one for the dog who sleeps the
most.

Toby was barking a lot last night, I think
that fox was around again but it won't come too
close.

Going with Rosie to the cinema tomorrow,
don't know what we'll be seeing yet.

Love Lillie xxx

*   *   *

'The first thing you should do - and this is very important - is not let the humans know you can get out of the shed.' Flame whispered as we made our way back towards the wood shed. 'If they know that then they'll probably block up the hole and you'll be trapped.'

I didn't like the sound of that, 'The mice will be trapped in there too,' I said worriedly. Flame sighed, 'What is it with you and squeaky snacks? Listen, mice can get in - and out - of anywhere, trust me. But *you* need to be able to get in and out don't you? So, make sure the humans never see you outside.'

That would be distressing for me and Flame; the comfort and security of the wood shed was nice, and especially the warmth, but not the thought of being stuck in there and never being able to see the sky or the Great Outside.

'Now, as I was saying, there's something you should do when the humans are not around. You must visit the chickens. I know they're birds, but you will understand them, they speak like us and they will tell you a lot about humans - and other things besides. The humans keep them and feed them just like they are doing with you; they are really odd creatures, but they will give you some good advice.'

We talked until the moon went down and then Flame bounded off to hunt while I returned to the woodshed thinking about what my friend had told me. Chickens?

I had never met a chicken, how could there be a bird that didn't fly? It would be like having a hedgehog that didn't walk.

There was food and a puddle as usual near my home and while the kindness of Whisper was most welcome, there was a part of me that missed hunting. It is, after all, what hedgehogs are designed to do. There is nothing quite as pleasurable as snuffling through the long grasses and weeds, beneath hedges, under bushes and around the roots of trees.

The food was good here but... ahhh, berries and slugs and worms, the gentle fall of a light summer rain while sheltering under a sweet-scented bush chatting with Patience as we waited for a gap in the showers; the sight of an owl passing across the face of the moon...

Recalling what Flame had said I promised myself never to get caught outside the wood shed... let's stay for the winter and then go home!

It was a big risk venturing out in the day to see if the humans were away. If they weren't then I might be caught and put back in the woodshed and they would hunt for the escape hole and block it.

So, on my first daylight expedition, I waited until Whisper had visited with food and then left. The bushes to the rear of the shed offered some cover before creeping around to the back of the human nest to see if the Moon-Eyed Beasts were there.

It was no good, the only way to check out the area properly would be to cross the path of small stones which took time and, in the full light of day, that meant it was possible to be seen from the human nest. I decided not to risk it and returned to the shed.

Then there came a thought so clever it might have been one of Flame's.

The dog hated being alone in the human nest and when they left he always called out the same things. 'Come back! Come back! Wait! Come back!' Before finally settling down and going to sleep; all that was necessary was to wait for him to call out and then it would be safe to leave the shed.

Sure enough, later that day when the sun had started its fall there came the sound of a Moon-Eyed Beast roaring and then, as the sound got fainter, the dog began calling out,

'Come Back! Wait! Don't leave me behind!'

Cautiously, I left the woodshed and headed out under the bushes, along the corner of the short grass and boldly across the path of small stones to the rear of the human nest. Sure enough, there were no Moon-Eyed Beasts there and so it was down to the rear of the house, passing under more fruit trees, and onward in the direction of the sound of chickens.

They really did look like birds, covered in feathers but they appeared too heavy to get off the ground. One flapped its wings but made no attempt to get into the air. They were closed in by a tall barrier of the woven human material that is impossible to chew through, which was also buried in the ground. This was probably to keep Flame and other foxes away from them.

On approaching the barrier, a number of the closest chickens immediately spotted me and trotted over to take a look. They were continually chattering away to each other and even before they had spoken to me it was obvious they were very quick-witted and intelligent creatures. I stopped at the barrier and listened to them discussing me as if I were not there.

'What do you suppose it is?

'It's a hedgehog.'

'White?'

'Indeed - rare thing in a hedgehog, whiteness.'

'I've never seen one before.'

'Neither have I, but my fourteenth great-grandmother did; saw two of them in fact, a brother and sister.'

'How fascinating, do you suppose it speaks?'

It seemed a good time to introduce myself. 'Hello, my name is Northwind.'

They all seemed to speak at once but still apparently understood each other.

'Well there's your answer.'

'Quite so, what a strange little creature.'

'Shall we speak to it?'

'I think Mater should.'

A chicken the same shade as Flame came as close to me as the barrier would allow.

'My name is Mater, I'm senior hen; do you live close to here?'

'I live in the wood shed,' I replied.

'Do you really? Well well; the wood shed? Do the humans know you are in there?'

'Yes, one of them has been feeding me and putting a puddle close by for me to drink. They have made me a sort of home.' This set off another lot of chattering.

I couldn't imagine how they made sense of it when they all spoke at once. Mater turned to me again, 'As far as I know hedgehogs do not lay eggs and you're too small to be even one human meal, so I'm assuming you're some kind of pet?'

'Pet?' I asked.

'Yes, yes - a pet, like the cat and dog; humans have creatures they call "pets," they don't eat them and the creatures don't produce anything useful. It seems that humans just enjoy seeing them.'

I must have sounded relieved, 'I was afraid they were going to eat me; are you pets too?'

Mater seemed to look at me for a long time before she answered;

'No... no we're not pets.'

Her head moved very quickly, as if she wanted to look at me from lots of different positions. It was scary until I realised it was just her way of seeing me with both eyes and building up a picture of what I really looked like.

When a chicken looks at you it is as if they are looking for all the things you haven't told them; they are trying to unearth all your secrets and all you might have to teach them. For them, life is one long lesson. And I was to discover they have one amazing power that no other walking creature has.

They remember everything.

*   *   *

14

Tell me Some More of Your Name

'Tell me some more of your name?' Mater demanded.

'I don't understand,' I told her, 'Northwind is all there is.'

The hen clucked and studied me with one sharp and curious eye.

'That is like a leaf saying there is nothing else when of course it is part of a big tree! I am called Mater but that's just the name for this tiny part of me. My full name is so long I would have to speak all through the winter just to say it!'

'I'm not sure I understand,' I told her. In fact, I didn't understand at all.

Mater frowned at a loose feather and quickly plucked it out. She turned her attention back to me.

'What are the names of your mother and father?'

That was something Mother and Dawn had taught me.

'My mother was called Rivermist and I think my father's name might have been Rainpuddle - but hedgehogs don't really know their fathers.'

She clucked approvingly, 'Well, that's a start - so you are Northwind of Rivermist and, possibly, Rainpuddle; now, what were the names of your mother's mother and father and your father's father and mother?'

It wasn't something I had ever thought about.

'I'm sorry, I know my mother's mother was called Dawn, the same as my sister - but that's all, no-one ever told me any more names.'

The chickens sounded amazed by this and set off in a stream of confused clucking and chatter which made little sense to me.

'Never told him?'

'Unbelievable!'

'He really doesn't know who he is?'

Mater walked along the other side of the barrier, 'Follow me,' she said and I scurried along trying to keep up with her. We left the other chickens still noisily discussing me and retreated to a quieter corner hidden by a thick and pleasantly-smelling bush. It felt safer there.

Mater settled down, 'Now then, I'll tell you a little more of my name, I am Mater of Firecomb and Yellowflower, Sawthorne and Bramble; of Coldsun and Runfar, Corn and Daymoon, of Luckwarm and Bran, Redspur and Rill, Nettlebreeze and Shy, Blue-Eye and Wormstrike, Lostmother and Tall, Newsun and Youngdock, Flood and Darkwings...'

'There are many, many, many more; I can name all those who live in me back through the countless winters to the time when it was always winter and to the time before that when there was no winter - that was a time before humans and hedgehogs and foxes; a time when my ancestors were big, very big; bigger than humans, even bigger than human nests and we ruled the Great Outside.'

'When we walked the ground shook and our roaring blew holes in the clouds. And I remember their names, Scarhand and Rainhunter, N'Grumm and Gronk, Kraktree and Bloodmoon... I remember them all because without them I would not be here.'

'I see...' I said, 'but I don't think I could remember all the hedgehogs that came before me, even if someone told me their names.'

Mater clucked gently, 'Of course not, you're not a chicken; no-one but chickens can do that. But you must never forget there are many who came before you so that you could be here.'

'I'll try to remember,' I assured her.

'Who sent you to find us?' Mater asked.

My reply seemed to surprise her, 'Flame the Fox, I told him I was going to spend the winter being cared for by the humans and he said the chickens would tell me useful things.'

'Were you surprised he didn't eat you?' Mater asked.

'Yes - but then he told me he would never eat a creature whose name he knew. He saved me from Zephyr the cat,' I told her.

Mater clucked a laugh, 'You see how important names are?' she said, '...well, Flame is correct, there ARE many things I can tell you about living close to humans, things that will help you survive, but, more importantly, I can tell you things about yourself. But not now - now you must go back to the wood shed. The humans will be returning. Come here tomorrow as soon as you hear the dog calling in the morning and we will have a long talk.'

But the dog did not make a sound the next morning. A Moon-Eyed Beast remained next to the human nest, cold and asleep. It was not until the following day that the dog called out for his humans to return.

It was a chilly and misty morning; the pale early sun was trying to peek through but clouds held her back. The leaves dripped with cold dew and spider webs hung between the branches of bushes.

I could hear the cries of big black birds passing overhead and understood only a few of their words. The smell of the recently departed Moon-Eyed Beast still hung in the air to the side of the human nest but I passed it by and made my way across the clinging wet grass to the edge of the chickens' area.

This time, I was no longer a novelty and most of them ignored me but Mater approached and I followed her to the spot she had shown me on my last visit. There was a question I wanted to ask.

'You know that Flame will not eat a creature if he knows its name? So why are you afraid of him?'

Mater chuckled, 'We're not afraid, just cautious. He is a hunter, he needs to eat, but he is clever and has always found enough food. He is also young, fit and strong so hunting comes easily to him.

When you have enough food, you can choose who and what to eat. That's why humans in this part of the Great Outside have creatures as pets; they do not know real hunger.'

Mater seemed to pause and look into the distance before continuing, 'Flame knows where we are, we cannot run or hide and if times got really hard he would try to eat us if he had to - whether he knows our names or not. Luckily, there are many, many rabbits.'

'I have seen a lot of rabbits but never met one,' I told her.

'Nor will you,' she replied, 'Rabbits speak only to rabbits, they trust no-one, but everything that a fox would otherwise eat is grateful to them. There is another reason why Flame would rather not eat chickens here; he likes these humans, they do not kill - even though they eat creatures that other humans have killed.'

'Flame knows that. All foxes - and most other creatures - quickly learn who they can trust and who they cannot. Humans here fed him in the cold of winter when food was hard to find. He will never forget their kindness.'

Mater scratched the cold damp earth and searched unsuccessfully for something edible in the soil.

'Should I trust these humans?' I asked her.

'Yes,' she replied, 'they will not harm you; they are among the good ones. There are three types of humans, Northwind; there are the good ones who are kind; there are the bad ones who are cruel and then there are the worst ones of all - the ones who don't care what the bad ones do - as long as they are not doing it to them.'

Despite what Flame had claimed, it now seemed likely that Mater was probably the cleverest creature I would ever meet. And just when I thought she had no more surprises she amazed me once more.

'The young human you call Whisper, her real name is...'
'*Lillie.*'

I must have looked astounded. 'How do you do that?' I asked.

Mater chuckled, 'Many birds can do it - human speech is just a matter of listening and repeating. Here's some more...

'*Come on... chick chick chick dinner time!*'

I laughed and then tried repeating the sounds for myself but couldn't make noises anything like that.

'Do you talk with humans?' I asked.

Mater clucked and fixed me with that strange chicken stare, 'No - I can copy their sounds but I haven't the faintest idea what most of them mean. Many birds imitate human speech but it's probably better if they don't know chickens can do it too. You see Northwind, humans admire intelligence in themselves and in creatures they control, but they fear it in anything else. We sometimes have fun with Zephyr by calling...'

'*Falstaff - puss puss puss!*'

'And he comes running and finds nobody here but us chickens.'

Mater had truly astonished me; birds are so clever. It was impossible for me to ever make human sounds even though I could hear them in my head.

I reached the hole in the back wall of the wood shed. Mater had warned me the humans were returning. Now the dog was calling out as the sound of the Moon-Eyed Beast grew louder;

'I am here... Where have you been...? I thought you were never returning... I am so relieved... I want a wee!'

There was much to think about and lots of new knowledge to digest. It seemed there was nothing Mater did not know. If you are a creature that remembers everything then all the wisdom of time is yours. And I had been told things I was sure no hedgehog before me ever knew.

For instance, Humans can live for ninety winters or more. I didn't fully understand what 'ninety' was, but apparently it was as long as a hedgehog lived, then another hedgehog, then another hedgehog, then another hedgehog, then another hedgehog, then another hedgehog, then another hedgehog, then another hedgehog, then another hedgehog, then another hedgehog, then another hedgehog, then another hedgehog, then another hedgehog, then another hedgehog and then another hedgehog!

Also, Mater said the dog is a type of fox - or a fox is a type of dog, I couldn't remember which, but dogs live as human pets. They never had to hunt but would never know real freedom. Cats were wild and clever, but they could be cruel and they could also become lazy when fed by humans.

Whisper was a young female human; she lived in the nest with her mother and father. Mater and her fellow chickens had been here for the past three winters. And I had nothing to fear, I was under the protection of the humans and so even Zephyr would not harm me.

But I still missed my old home and yearned to get back to it.

Mostly, I learned that one lifetime, whatever creature you are, is just not long enough to discover all the amazing things there are to find out. Mater had spoken human words; sounds I could think but never say.

The Great Outside - what humans called *'The World'* - was full of wonders.

*   *   *

October 16th
Cloudy and damp.

I don't know what Rosie sees in Michael Brown, he listens to rubbish music and wears stupid shoes – and he boasts about how much they cost. I told him if I spent that much on a pair of shoes they would at least look nice!

She is going bowling with him tomorrow. It's not a proper bowling arena like we had in the city, just an alley in the lounge of The Unicorn where there is some sort of party going on.

I don't care, Mum said we can go to the city again next weekend to stay overnight and see Nan and Granddad – and I can catch up with my REAL friends!!!

Exciting times for Jack though. We had a visit just as I came home from school; a reporter called Nina and a photographer called Nick from The Bugle came to write a story all about Jack. They thought he was beautiful and he posed for the camera like a real celebrity. I can't wait to see him in the paper!

He is a happy little chappy and grunts and squeaks to me now when I visit him as if he knows me.

He keeps himself very clean and always looks forward to his treats. He is growing quite quickly but Dad says it is unlikely he will be able to hibernate this winter as hedgehogs need to weigh at least 450 grams in order to survive the long sleep; ideally they should be 600 grams and Jack only weighs 432. Besides, it's warm in the wood shed so he may well decide to stay awake.

This diary belongs to: Lillie Marsh

Mum's play went really well, everyone enjoyed it. Dad wasn't there, he couldn't get home from work but they filmed the whole thing so he will be able to see it when he gets back.

Good night diary (and goodnight Jack, and Toby, and Falstaff) xxx

(P.S. And Mum's hens: Regan, Goneril, Cordelia, Juliet, Ophelia and Viola).

* * *

15

Dawn

It is the size of humans that still makes me feel uncomfortable with them. The ones I have met do not want to hurt me, but they are so large if one of them squeezed me too hard or dropped me from such a height it could badly injure me. I like meeting them, however, because they do the strangest things.

One day the door to the woodshed opened and Whisper entered. This was usual but when three other humans came in behind her I was very curious to discover why. One of the humans was Whisper's mother. Mater the chicken had told me humans were good at sharing ideas with each other and these were making noises which grew louder, but not in any way scary, when they saw me.

I had been for a drink when they came in and my first instinct was to scurry back in and hide but that might have made one of them lift the roof off, which is still disturbing. And so, I just stood and looked up at them as they approached.

To have four humans all looking at you at once is an odd thing, Whisper kneeled down and gently picked me up, raising me higher and higher until it seemed big human eyes were everywhere. I looked from one face to the other; such big eyes and strange scents.

They stayed for what seemed like a long time, one of them got really close to me while hiding behind a strange human thing (The disguise did not work, I could still see the human) and eventually they left and all was quiet in the wood shed again except for the tiny squeaks of a new family of mice who are living in one of the wood piles.

The days were getting colder, the nights were getting longer and there was less and less daylight, just like Mother had told us. I was leaving the woodshed only at night now, afraid of discovery outside in the daylight. Flame visited regularly and kept me informed about life in the Great Outside and all the places that had once been home.

And that very night he came again. Somewhere an owl was calling its mate far away in the woods and a pair of mice had left earlier; I hoped they would be safe out there. They were probably heading for the chickens because lots of suitable food for mice lay around that area.

Flame would not eat them, he had been told they were my friends, but that owl and others might be hunting - as well as Zephyr who would certainly not let a mouse get away from him again!

'Hey, Frosty-Face; come on out, I've got a surprise for you!' Flame's whisper came from outside and I scurried off behind the wood pile to the escape-hole. Squeezing through (I realised I was growing - either that or the hole was somehow getting smaller) I popped out into the Great Outside and the fresh night air.

Flame was sitting close to the sweet-smelling bush. Above us, the tall tree whose branches stretched over the woodshed was looking more and more bare, its leaves falling to earth as winter marched closer. Crossing the flattened long grass and tired old dandelions I joined my friend.

'So what is this surprise?' I asked. There was a lot to tell him about my meetings with Mater and the visit by the group of humans but his surprise was really... surprising. He grinned and called over his shoulder:

'Come on out!'

From behind him a hedgehog appeared, and my heart leapt with delight.

'Dawn' I cried, squealing with real joy.

We rubbed noses, 'Oh Northwind - you really are safe and well,' she sounded tired but happy and somehow... older. She had of course grown but was still unmistakeably my clever sister.

'Flame told me where you were and I have walked such a long way to see you - you have grown so big, is it true the humans are feeding you?'

Flame interrupted before I could respond. 'I met her at the edge of the woods, I was just about to... well, you know, then she said - quick as anything, "I am called Dawn!"

I thought to myself, "I wonder where she learned that trick?" so I asked her, "Not related to a white hedgehog by any chance, are you?" Then I told her where you were and escorted her here.'

'Dawn, I'm so pleased to see you!' I said.

There is so much happiness in simply seeing a familiar face and discovering a much-loved and missed scent, it was hard to stop looking at her and smiling. Not only was she my sister but she was also the first other hedgehog I had seen for what seemed a very long time. We had so much catching up to do.

Flame yawned, 'I'm not going to waste what's left of a fine night listening to hedgehogs waffling on about slugs they have nibbled, I'm off to hunt,' he turned to Dawn, 'I'll come back for you and see you safely across the road later' and with a flashing smile he was off through the hedge and heading in the direction of the woods.

'Have you heard from Rain and Puddle?' I asked, wondering where my brothers' travels might have taken them.

Dawn frowned briefly then offered a sad smile.

'Rain is well I believe. There is another big field behind our nest and he lives on the other side of that. We haven't met for some time though. As for Puddle... he went hunting in the woods and... I warned him there were many badgers there...'

She didn't have to explain further. 'Poor Puddle,' I said sadly. 'He never did listen, did he?'

'But, look at you,' Dawn brightened, '...what a big hedgehog you've become!'

We talked well into the night, I told her about Whisper the Human and about Mater the chicken and all the things I had learned from the wise old bird. I told her what a good friend Flame was and she cheered me a lot when she informed me that Patience the wood mouse was still alive and well and often asked about me.

But it became clear as we talked that we now lived in different worlds. As she told me how difficult it was to find food some nights for both hunters and hunted because the Great Outside was getting colder, I felt a little bit guilty that I was safe in a warm shed where my food and drink was supplied to me.

'Stay here, stay with me Sister...' I urged, '...these humans are good ones who are kind to hedgehogs, kind to all things. You'll be safe and warm and will never be hungry.'

She smiled, 'I can't Brother, I belong out there across the field, it will always call me back as I know it still calls to you - but we are different. I am the colour of the dark hedges and the twigs and dying ferns. I am hard to see. Don't worry about me - I will be going into the deep sleep soon in the old home and when I wake it will be warm again. I'll try to visit you then.'

As the first light of the new day turned the sky from black to a muddy grey behind the human nest Flame returned as promised. I rubbed noses with my sister...

'Take care Dawn, I will be thinking about you.'

'You take care too my handsome, wintry Brother; when the warmth comes again maybe we will both become parents.'

And with Flame leading, I watched as Dawn shuffled through the hedge while the fox checked the lane for Moon-Eyed Beasts. I heard him tell her it was safe to cross and then I heard her calling out,

'Stay safe Northwind.'

'I will, I promise,' I called back.

One day she would become a wise mother just like ours and would lead her hoglets out on that first magical night to see the moon and twinkles hanging in the vast sky above the Great Outside; but I also knew something else while shuffling tiredly into the wood shed for a sleep.

Hedgehogs get so wrapped up in their busy night to night lives they have little time for friends and relations. It was only because life was so easy here with the humans that there was time to think of things apart from where my next slug or berry was coming from.

Dawn would always love me, as I would always love her - but we both also knew we would never meet again.

*   *   *

October 28th

Fog and then sunny but chilly.

Jack is in the local paper!

He is also on the Bugle's website and I have posted the link on my timeline so all my friends in the city can see him. Lots of people have 'liked' him so far.

He has put on a lot of weight this last couple of weeks and Lindsey from County Hedgehog Rescue says he might be able to hibernate after all but may well not want to as we are keeping him in a safe warm place.

Jack's a white prickly fellow!

By Nina Mason

A local girl's one in ten thousand chance encounter with a white hedgehog has been the talk of her school - and her online blog where the story has now received more than 1,000 hits.

Lillie Marsh, 13, of Cherry Hill Cottage found the young hedgehog in her garden late one evening recently; she thinks it had been hunting and was scared by the family cat, Falstaff and the presence of a nearby fox.

She has named the new arrival 'Jack' because, she says, he reminded her of 'Jack Frost' and now plans to care for him until he reaches maturity.

Wildlife expert, Lindsey Keith, of County Hedgehog Rescue stated,

● **Rare white hedgehog, Jack has found a safe home**

'Albino hedgehogs are very rare, just one in ten thousand births are all white with distinctive pink eyes. In the wild it is very unlikely that Jack would have survived without a hedgehog's natural camouflage.'

As for Jack, he is set to spend a cosy winter in his purpose-built home.

With a healthy diet of tinned dog food, clean water and TLC he is already putting on weight and, far from being a prickly customer, he seems happy and content in his new surroundings

Nina, the reporter, wrote a lovely story about him. I am going to the Bugle's offices later this week as it is half-term and Nina said I can sit and watch them putting the pages of The Bugle together on screen. I have also been speaking to Lindsey and I am going to write a news story about how to make gardens friendly for hedgehogs by leaving holes in fences so they can come and go and not using netting and most importantly making sure there are no hedgehogs in piles of leaves and things before setting fire to them. There are less than one million hedgehogs left in the country – there are more humans in the City than that!

*   *   *

16

The North Wind Is Here

Darkness was falling when I woke; eating and drinking reminded me how lucky I was not to have to risk everything for it. At this time Dawn would be out there on the far side of the field preparing to go out and hunt, facing danger to find food.

It had been so good to see her. Hedgehogs are solitary creatures but with such an unusual life as mine it was nice to be reminded that somewhere in the Great Outside were relatives who still remembered me.

Even so, there was still Mater and the hens to talk to as well as regular visits from Flame and Whisper. Her human words were impossible to understand, but it was simple to sense her kindness.

And so, my days and nights drifted past in a time of learning, sleeping, eating and drinking and chatting with the various creatures passing through what Mater had told me was the garden of the human nest; this is an area that for some reason humans build or grow barriers around and then imagine it belongs to them.

Then began the change.

I could feel it in the air. It was a special day, a day for laughing, scurrying and chasing leaves. A day full of promise.

I first felt it when I was out and about in the middle of the afternoon, having of course made sure the humans were not at home.

Normally, if a hedgehog is seen in daylight, especially so close to winter, there is something wrong with them and they need help. But my patterns of waking and sleeping were much different.

This was a lively day, a day for jumping up and down and scurrying in all directions just for the fun of it!

Mater had sensed the change too, there had been a shift in the wind and it was much colder. She looked up at the sky, turning her head quickly to see as much of it as she could.

'North wind,' she said.

'Yes?' I replied, and she laughed.

'No, no, not Northwind... north wind!'

I must have looked confused.

She clucked and sighed, '...the wind... it's coming from the north - it's a north wind. Winter is here.'

I looked up at the sky behind the human nest and I saw first one, then another... and another... tiny falling flakes of white.

'Here it comes,' another hen had joined us in looking up.

'Is the whole of the Great Outside going to turn white?' I asked excitedly.

'As white as you,' Mater replied.

But not that day; there was just a little bit of snow, a taste of what was to come. It settled on the roof of the human nest and in the corners of the garden and around the bases of the trees but everything else stayed autumn dark. It was colder though and over the next few days thicker and darker clouds came out of the north and it got colder still.

It was my first experience of winter and while Mater had told me much about what to expect, she had always had the chicken shed to live in and humans to feed her.

Mother too had told us of this time but had slept through her winters. I needed someone to tell me about what winter really meant to those who lived through it. But there had been no visit from Flame for several days and I was beginning to wonder if he was well.

On a bright and very cold morning when, for the first time, I saw a frozen puddle, I waited until the sun rose higher before leaving the woodshed. I had remained inside all night listening to the wind and waiting in vain for a call from my friend. Now, as noon passed clouds were once more coming from the north; thick and dark, brooding as if weary of the great load they carried.

Where could he be? I reminded myself he was a very clever fox and good at taking care of himself, but... It was simply not like him to stay away for so long. And when a possible answer did come, it was from an unexpected source - and deeply worrying.

'Still no sign of the wild dog?'

Zephyr's voice startled me. He was sitting on a low branch of the tree near the wood shed as if waiting for me.

Even under human protection, it never felt completely safe when Zephyr was around. He was a cat after all and, as Mater had once told me, all hunters become dangerous when their stomachs are empty - but cats plan ahead!

Zephyr dropped gracefully from the branch and padded to my side, studying me lazily with half-open eyes.

'Have you heard anything about Flame?' I asked.

The cat sniffed the air and looked thoughtfully at me before answering.

'Might have, might have indeed; tell me - do you know what a hunt is?'

'Of course,' I replied, a little confused, 'I hunted before coming to live here, all hedgehogs hunt.'

Zephyr chuckled but there was no warmth in it.

'I'm sure they do - in their own clumsy way, but I'm talking about a hunt by humans.'

'Humans... hunting?' This was a surprise to me.

'Yes, everything hunts in some way, even rabbits hunt for food and so it stands to reason doesn't it? Humans eat so therefore they have to go out and find the things they need to survive. Even so a few of them do it just for fun.'

'You mean, play-hunting - like hoglets and... young cats?' I asked.

'Sort of,' Zephyr replied, '...but these are grown humans who don't know what hunger is.'

I was puzzled, 'But that doesn't make sense?'

The cat stretched and yawned, 'Yes, well they're not the brightest of creatures - otherwise I would be feeding them and not the other way around. Anyway, the thing is, the fools have been hunting... got a fox so I hear.'

I felt a chill run through me; something both heavy and cold settled in my stomach and my legs trembled.

'What... what will they do to him?'

Zephyr shuddered and frowned and I'm sure I detected a hint of pity in those usually cold eyes.

'More than I would,' he said softly, and as he padded away he turned and added, '...and I'm a cat.'

It was the long-remembered lessons of my Mother that caused me to eat and drink my fill before following the only course of action that lay open to me. My friend was out there somewhere and, just as I had once done for Patience, there was no alternative but to try and find him. Even so, there was little that a single hedgehog could really do.

Leaving the wood shed and heading for the line of bushes that edged the garden reminded me this would be the first time I had crossed the path of the Moon-Eyed Beasts since coming here, which now seemed such a long time ago. The light was fading, partly due to the heavy afternoon clouds now crowding out the pale sun.

It was much too cold to be out and all my instincts were telling me to go back to the warmth and safety of the wood shed. Maybe Flame would visit tonight and all would be well. But Zephyr's story had left me deeply worried and so through the bushes I went and found myself on the side of the lane.

It was silent, even so it was wise to listen as hard as possible, knowing just how fast these beasts could appear; but with no sounds to worry about I set off and made it safely to the other side. In an instant I was through another hedge and standing on the edge of the great field.

Something cold and white landed on my nose before turning to water; I looked around and up at the sky which had now turned frighteningly dark, like a bottomless puddle.

172

Birds screamed as the wind tossed them like dry leaves.

Snow was falling, much more than on the first occasion. Big fat flakes dropping slowly to the ground. This time it looked as if the Great Outside really was going to turn white. But for once my lack of colour was going to work in my favour. It would be difficult for any hungry badger to spot me.

But it was so, so cold. My plan was to try and reach my old home and see if Dawn was there, if so maybe she had heard something about Flame; but before even reaching the half way point of the field there was snow under my feet; and still it fell, thicker and faster.

It was no longer possible to easily see one direction from another. The wind grew angrier and was so icy it hurt. Walking through snow was much harder than bare earth and it was a struggle to get anywhere.

The cold was making it difficult to think, it hurt my eyes and I longed to close them. Looking behind me, the hedge seemed so far away and the lights from the human nest were only barely visible in the distance twinkling through the snow storm.

There was no way to make it back and so the only thing to do was go on; but which way? Darkness had come quickly thanks to the thick clouds and the little hill on the far side of the field had disappeared into the murky night.

Walking directly away from the lights of the human nest and travelling only by memory and instinct each step was a struggle as my legs sank into the snow, making them colder and colder.

There was no longer any feeling in my feet and it seemed as if every spine had turned to ice. It was a struggle to simply think now. Where was I going? Why was I out at this terrible and dangerous time when hedgehogs were supposed to be asleep somewhere warm and safe? Something to do with a fox...?

Then the struggle stopped. There is a point when you become so cold you can no longer feel anything. Curling myself into a ball and no longer knowing or caring where I was or why, I surrendered to the mighty north wind whose name had become mine. Perhaps it would carry me to Mother and a safe warm nest... hoglets... Mother's milk... safety.

The whole of the Great Outside was going to sleep. And from somewhere, it seemed everywhere, a deep and ageless voice whispered to me in a way I could no longer resist. 'Sleep... North... wind...'

*　　*　　*

December 10th

Very cold. Freezing wind. Forecast snow.

Been with Mum to town to get bread and milk and all sorts of supplies. Lots of people had the same idea and the supermarket was very busy. Everyone says a blizzard is coming. I'm so glad we have plenty of wood in the woodshed. I'm glad Jack is safe and warm in there too. I feel so sorry for all the creatures out there in the woods that have to fight to survive in the winter.

Even Falstaff is staying indoors and he loves to be out and about. Toby just sleeps nowadays, he is very old.

Dad was due to go away for a meeting tomorrow but it looks as if he will have to do it online. We are almost two miles out of town and if we get heavy snow we may be cut off

*   *   *

17

Winter

'She is a beautiful! No other word for it!'

'Watching her drinking on the riverbank, occasionally turning to look at me and smile before trotting away into the woods, knowing I will follow her, makes my heart sing. I forget everything when we are together and even though it has only been a week... how could I ever live without her?'

'I even forgot winter was here until we left the woods and saw the snow falling heavily. The great field was already white; but we have a den.'

'Her name is Fern and now she is going back to the safety and warmth of the den while I hunt for us. The wild ducks have all gone to another part of the Great Outside where it doesn't snow, luckily there are always rabbits. You would think rabbits would sleep through the winter like hedgehogs but no, the big-eared fools are still up and about!'

'Talking of hedgehogs, I had better pop along and see Northwind soon. Now there's a sensible hedgehog; warm, well-fed, probably fast asleep dreaming of slugs or something while I'm out here on the edge of this field.'

"By my brush, it's cold!"

'I'll be lucky to catch anything tonight, I can hardly see - and I've got probably the best eyesight around these parts. I'll try behind Hedgehog Hill; there are bushes and a bit of shelter from this wind. Ha! I'll bet Northwind now knows why he was given his name.'

'Why can't we walk on our hind legs like humans? At least our front feet wouldn't get so cold then. I tried it once but fell over...'

'Come on rabbits, where are you? Just one - as long as it's a big one. You think they'd be glad to be eaten; it's warmer inside me than it is out here.'

'Even the scents are frozen out, I can't... wait... there is something... scents move so quickly in this wind it's hard to catch... ah – there it is again, not a rabbit though.'

'Still anything is better than... it's... it's a hedgehog I think. What would a hedgehog be doing out in winter? It is though, I'm sure it is. I'm rarely wrong, I've got the best nose in the whole of the...'

"...Northwind?"

"NORTHWIND! What...?"

'He's here, he's close, somewhere in this field... but the scent is being thrown around by the wind. What is the fool doing out in... I can't see for the snow and it's pitch black... but I can do this, I'm the cleverest fox in the whole of... there it is... this way... ah, yes... getting stronger. Snow - he's under this... oh no... please no.'

'Dig, just below the snow here and... prickles... the same colour as the snow.'

"Northwind..."

"NORTHWIND, CAN YOU HEAR ME?"

'Dig the snow from around him, he's so... cold. Not moving... Ohh... oh no...'

'Oh you silly, silly hedgehog, what were you doing out here? Please don't let it be that you were looking for me. I'm not going to cry... no I'm not, I'm the bravest fox in... in... I know what happened. I bet he heard about my Uncle Star, I bet that cat told him... told him it was me...'

'What a brave little friend you were Northwind, I will never... ever...'

'Wait... that's a heartbeat! The smallest and weakest heartbeat I've ever heard - but a heartbeat! Bless these brilliant ears! Dig Flame, come on... DIG! Clear a piece of ground, clear the snow off the grass... there now...'

"Northwind... can you hear me? Come on I'm going to lie down here and wrap myself around you and hold you up off the... OWW, prickles and try and keep you... AAAGH... you spiky little... OUCH... wrap you up and get you some warmth. My body warmth will keep you from... ARRGH! Flatten your spines you fool, I'm trying to be a life saver here and... OWWW! I'm glad my father can't see me now. By my brush it's cold."

"I'm not going to let you die little friend - even if it kills me!"

* * *

December 11th

JACK HAS GONE!!!

There is lots and lots of snow, but JACK IS NOT IN HIS NEST!!!

I looked around but can't find him anywhere. Dad helped me search and he says that perhaps Jack has found a way into one of the piles of logs and is hibernating in there. He surely wouldn't have gone out through the hole in this weather?

He says we must take extra care when collecting logs for the fire so as not to disturb the rest of the pile.

I tried calling Lindsey at County Rescue but she is not answering, perhaps her phone line is down, a lot are so I hear.

Why didn't he just hibernate in his nest? He seemed to like it in there. I've got a horrid feeling that he is somewhere out there in the snow. There was so much of it last night. I knew there had been lots when I woke this morning. I was lying in bed and there was silence.

No cars or tractors going past on the lane. We are cut off, there is at least a foot of snow on the lane and the whole world is white.

Dad is stuck here and I can't get to school. Mum phoned the school to tell them and they said a lot of children from out of town are going to be absent today.

Oh Jack – I wish I knew where you were. I know the fire brigade have machines that can detect body heat to find people who are trapped, I wish I had one. I will look again after breakfast; maybe carefully move some of the logs.

*   *   *

Was I alive?

I had to be, I was thinking! Everything was dark, but something told me it was daylight.

Then I suddenly realised; this was a nest - but not my own nest. What was going on? This was unlike any other nest I had ever been in. It was cosy and yet there was still a chill inside as If I had been somewhere so cold it would take forever to feel warm again.

And there was something else unusual about this nest; it was full of the scent of fox!

A horrible thought struck me - had I been eaten by a fox and was now inside one? No, that was ridiculous; if I had been eaten I wouldn't be thinking about it now. Then the memories began to return; the snow, the darkness, the terrible cold. I had been out in winter looking for... Flame – FLAME! That's who I could smell, all around me. I struggled to find a way out. Was I dreaming? Then a voice told me I was very much awake.

'OWWW! ...ARGGH Stop wriggling you prickly fool! YAAGH!'

'Flame...? Is that you?'

'Ah - so you're awake are you? I'm so glad!'

I put my head out and saw a completely different Great Outside to any I had seen before.

'Ohhh...' It was all I could say. There was a stillness all across the glittering white land; it was as if the whole of the Great Outside was holding its breath, waiting for something awesome to happen.

'Yes...,' said Flame, '...winter that is, and only an idiot - or a hero - would spend the night outside in it.'

'You... saved me!'

Now it all came back, my desperate struggle across the field trying to find my friend - and just how difficult it is to walk over snow and just how quickly the fierce cold could sap energy.

'I did,' Flame confirmed, '...and you've no idea how cold I now am - or... perhaps you have.'

'Zephyr told me there had been a hunt' I explained, 'and I was concerned.'

Flame smiled and licked snow off my nose with a warm tongue. His breath turned to icy clouds in the sharp morning air.

'There was a hunt, they got my Uncle Star; he was old. They would never have got me, the fools. Anyway, what were you planning to do to them? Scurry up the horses' legs and prick their noses or something?'

'I had to know,' I said.

'Well what we need to know now my friend is how are we going to get you back to safety? You are too prickly to carry, it's too far for you to walk and I can't stay here any longer or I'll be as frozen as you were.'

Flame stood up and without his warmth it soon began to feel bitingly cold again. He turned to me, his eyes dancing as if an idea too big for his mind was struggling to get out.

'Do you know, I'm sometimes so clever I even surprise myself; wait here!'

With a bound he was off across the snow in the direction of the woods. I began to shake with cold. In the daylight it was clear how far away the human nest was and just how unlikely it was that a hedgehog would make it back without help; but then Flame returned. He was carrying a piece of wood which he dropped at my feet on the small patch of grass he had cleared to sleep in.

'Ugh, tastes awful, do you know rabbits chew this stuff in the winter? Now then I want you to wrap your little legs around this and hold on tight, I know you can do it because I once saw a hedgehog climb a barrier that was taller than a fully-grown human, it was like the ones around the chicken area - you know the type? I was so impressed, I almost didn't eat him! Come on, grip hard and do NOT let go, are you listening?'

I did as Flame asked, not fully understanding what he planned to do but it became obvious when he picked the piece of wood up with me clinging tightly to it, his large white teeth almost touching my front legs and his hot breath on my face as he started out towards the human nest and safety.

I watched the snow-covered ground speeding beneath us as Flame trotted and hopped across the white blanket. Now and then he sank so deep that his legs completely disappeared and he had to leap into the air to get back out. When he did this, I had to hold on very tightly indeed.

Soon we were at the line of bushes; I almost fell off the wood as we pushed through. There was no need to look for Moon-Eyed Beasts today; their track was covered in deep snow.

As we passed through the far hedge and into the human garden Whisper was standing at the rear of the shed, it was clear by the way she was studying the corner under the tree that she had discovered the hole through which I passed in and out of my home.

Flame stopped with me still clinging to the piece of wood in his jaws. It was obvious to him too that there was no way for me to get into the warmth and safety of the shed without being spotted. I thought he would put me down and make his escape but instead he did the most incredible thing.

He trotted forward, Whisper turned and spotted us, she was clearly shocked. Flame advanced towards her and stopped a few paces away and then gently put the wood on the snowy ground. I let go and stretched my aching legs, looking between the fox and the human who were studying each other is silence. Flame spoke softly and quickly.

'I'll be back to see you soon, you are safe now.'

And my amazing, brave and clever friend turned and bounded away, back through the fence toward the frozen fields.

*　　*　　*

18

What Do We Never Do To Friends?

t was still as warm as summer in the human nest and for the next two days and nights it became my nest too.

It was a place where night and day begin suddenly thanks to indoor suns that shine for humans whenever they choose. It is a place where it never seems to rain and yet there is water.

There were drinks that tasted of berries, then, when the warmth had fully returned to my body, Whisper took me back out to the woodshed where my nest was full of fresh dry leaves and hay. When she left I added my own little touches and made it comfortable.

Soon there was a cosy chamber that wrapped around me and held me as Mother once had, and all I wanted to do was curl up in the warmth and close my eyes. Dreams came then, images of the great white wilderness outside; of Flame and Whisper and Mater and all who would be living through the cruel cold.

Deeper and deeper into sleep, falling down a tunnel that got warmer and softer, ending in a place where there were no dreams at all and time stopped.

Everything beyond my nest ceased to exist; there was only my little bed of leaves floating in darkness until, after a time impossible to measure, the dreams returned. They were dreams of food and puddles, hunger and thirst. I stretched and yawned and stood up, my legs were surprisingly wobbly but I also felt refreshed.

The air seemed warmer and on a gentle southern breeze that crept under the door of the shed came the scent of leaves and young grass. There were no food or puddle dishes but that was nothing to worry about, Whisper often took them away and returned them cleaned and full again. But then I looked around... stopped and blinked and looked again... unable to make sense of what I saw.

The shed was empty; the great piles of wood had disappeared!

* * *

Ce est le journal de

Mademoiselle Lillie Marsh

Avril 16

Chaud et ensoleillé
Jacques Hérisson est éveillé (Jack the
Hedgehog is awake !)

I went into the woodshed this morning
planning to take the lid off the hedgehog house
to check on him, but he was outside walking
about looking a bit confused. I brought him some
food and water and he tucked in straight away.

. . . je me souviens . . .

He must have been starving after such a long sleep but it's so good to see him alive and well, particularly after his winter scare.

Lindsey says he probably wouldn't have hibernated under normal circumstances but that the deep cold and shock of his 'adventure' tricked his ~~metabullism metabow~~ body into thinking it was too cold to stay awake.

The fox brought him back, I know it did. It could so easily have killed him but it didn't. We have fed it all through the winter and it is now a regular visitor.

It's a dog fox and I have named him Flame and now when I call to him sometimes he comes through the hedge to me.

I wish I could put into words how it felt that moment when Flame dropped Jack by my feet, still clinging to that branch, and then looked up at me. Our eyes met and it was the most strange and amazing thing like... I don't know, communicating with an alien or something.

I have been to France with the school, we saw the Bayeux Tapestry and ate in a pavement café. I bought Dad a tee-shirt and Mum a book of photographs and I got myself this diary or journal.

France is really cool and tres chic. I wonder would Jack mind if I changed his name to Jacques? He is a 'hérisson' in French.

. . . je me souviens . . .

Perhaps I should call him Jacques Hérisson (or Jack Harrison) ? LOL !

The hole in the shed is a bit small for him now, so we have blocked it off to stop him hurting himself and we have created a bigger hatch at the rear of the shed so that he can pass in and out during the summer.

I am no longer afraid the fox (Flame) is going to hurt him and it is cruel to keep him inside when he wants to wander and do natural hedgehog things. We will keep an eye on him however and check him very often to make sure he doesn't wander too far.

Toby is very old, he has trouble walking, he is now thirteen and Dad says that is a good innings for a Basset.

Falstaff does not seem to get older, just plumper and lazier but he is a happy cat most of the time. Also, Cordelia, our senior hen, has sadly passed away.

She had stopped laying a long time ago but Mum said she could live out her days with us. She was really intelligent and I'm sure she listened to me when I talked to her.

Bonne Nuit – bien dormir tous les mondes xx

*　　*　　*

The great winter, my first, was over. The terrible snow had gone and warmth was returning to the ground.

Mornings were damp and misty; the moisture hung on spiders' webs and in little bubbles of water from the fence surrounding the chicken run. The sun rose from the field earlier every day and took longer to pass across the sky before falling behind the hill to the rear of the human nest.

Whisper was bringing food and puddles again but there was another shock. It was not a surprise to discover the hole in the shed through which I had passed in and out on my travels had been blocked, but nearby there was another hole, this one bigger and in the kind of shape humans make - there was human scent around it. Whisper, or one of the other humans, had clearly made this hole in the knowledge that I would use it to come and go.

There is a small time of day before the chickens retire for the night and hedgehogs are awake. At this time I headed for the chicken run to visit Mater. The sun had disappeared behind the hill and the birds in the skies were all shouting at once about where they planned to sleep. It was a different hen who approached the wire.

'Ah - the white hedgehog; Northwind of Rivermist and Rainpuddle and Dawn and "I-don't-know-the-rest" isn't it?'

'That's right,' I replied, '...where is Mater?'

'Her name is still here but the rest of her has gone,' the bird replied.

'I am Blue-Eye of Darkfeather and Curious and Dream and Sleeplate and... well, I won't bother telling you the rest, you'd only forget. I am head chicken now; if you were a friend of Mater's then you're a friend of mine too.'

I was sorry to hear I would never see Mater again but Blue-Eye told me the old hen had enjoyed a long and happy life. She also told me the dog was very old and never left the human nest any more. I had never really got to know him, not even his name. All he had ever done was shout at me when we met.

'I'm on guard! I'm on guard!'

Zephyr had said all dogs were fools but Flame was a sort of dog and certainly no fool.

But with the old dog remaining inside the human nest it did mean that Flame was now visiting the garden quite a lot according to Blue-Eye who was naturally very wary of him, although he had assured her he was not going to attack any of the chickens.

The humans were apparently feeding him and he was, of course, clever enough not to do anything that would stop this.

There was no visit from Flame that day, or the next. In fact it was several days after waking that my friend finally appeared. I was heading out for an evening patrol and found him waiting just outside the shed under the overhanging tree.

'Ha - so you've finally woken up?' He looked thinner, but well.

'Flame,' I smiled, 'It's so good to see you.'

'Likewise,' he replied, 'I hope you were warm and cosy while I was bravely battling the snow and frost to feed me and my better half?'

'Your what?' I was puzzled.

Flame beamed, 'Ahh she's beautiful - her name's Fern.'

'You've got a mate?' I laughed.

'Got more than a mate,' he answered - '...want to see something amazing?' He turned and gave a quick bark and two small cubs crept from under the hedge and approached us on wobbly legs.

'This one is Flame, named after me and this other one is Fern, named after her mother.'

They were delightful, they circled me curiously wagging their tiny tails and sniffing at my spines. One got a prick on the nose and gave a small yelp.

'I warned you,' Flame told the tiny cub, '...he's a hedgehog, they are very prickly. This is Northwind, my friend - and if we know someone's name what is it we never do?'

'We never eat them,' the cubs answered together.

I laughed, 'They're beautiful.'

'They are indeed,' agreed Flame, 'In fact - and I never thought I would say this - I'm probably not the handsomest fox in the Great Outside anymore!'

Flame took his cubs back to their den far across the field, he promised to visit again very soon. It was after he had gone, during that silent time of evening when the birds have finally fallen asleep, the insects have retired and the night hunters are still half awake that I realised all the things I was going to miss as a long summer stretched before me.

Hunting by moonlight, sniffing and wandering beneath the hedges and maybe making a nest of my own; and all because of my wintry white shade.

I was sadly aware that the dangers to me were greater than those faced by dark hedgehogs like Dawn and just making it through the season would be highly unlikely out there in the wild.

Flame was not the only fox in those woods and there were plenty of other creatures who would see me as food rather than a friend. The safest place was surely right here among the humans, but there was still the longing for the natural life I would never lead.

In days to come I would look back on that summer as a time of wistfully watching others doing what came naturally. Both of Flame's lovely cubs made it through that season, I learned much more about the Great Outside and the creatures in it from Blue-Eye. And Whisper continued to care for me.

There were happy days as the wood piles began to grow again in the shed and a new family of mice moved in, their busy chatter and activity were endlessly entertaining; and there were days of sadness too. The old dog left only his name behind and Whisper was very sad.

And Flame brought to me the tragic news that brave little Patience the wood mouse who survived two winters had been taken by an owl; another reminder of how cruel the Great Outside could be.

Zephyr the cat became friendlier to me in his own stand-offish way and as the seasons turned, I too turned, into a fully-grown hedgehog and promised myself that after another winter it would be time to do all that a hedgehog should do.

The season of growing passed and summer turned once again to the time of change when the leaves fell, the days got shorter and chilly mists rolled across the field and through the human garden chilling the tired dandelions and leaving glittering drops of water on the chicken's fence and spiders webs.

When winter returned, I looked up at the moon hanging in the icy sky as clouds, chased by the north wind, brought a deadly white cloak to cast over the Great Outside and bring back the time of hardship and struggle.

Next summer would be full of promise.

*   *   *

19

Breeze & the Badger

There is a new dog at the human nest, a male cub and very playful. He took a few prickles to the nose while trying to get to know me but soon became a regular sight in the garden.

His name is Black Ear although the humans, of course, make one of their noises when they wish to call to him. He is even friendly to Flame and enjoys nothing more than sitting and listening to the Fox's tales of great hunts, brave and cunning deeds and all the wonders of the Great Outside.

It had rained but as night began to fall, the clouds cleared allowing the bright twinkle which hedgehogs call the Hunters' Light to glitter in the sky behind the human nest.

Sometimes the Hunters' Light shows itself at the start of the night and at other times it waits until dawn is breaking. It is the brightest light in the sky except for the sun and moon of course.

Little buds of rain water still hung from the leaves and twigs of the hedge and dropped on to me as I disturbed them on my way through. Whisper still fed me but there was also a need to hunt and explore - and now there were other feelings which were difficult to describe.

I had passed through two winters and was fully-grown. Things now felt different and without anyone telling me, it was clear what a hedgehog of my age should be seeking.

It was almost completely dark when the call came, it was the kind of call I had never heard before but instantly knew I had to answer. It came again, from somewhere out in the gloom, a call as old as the far past that Mater and Blue-Eye had taught me about. A call a hedgehog could no more resist than food or drink.

I headed off in the direction of the sound which took me along the edge of the human garden and into the long and untamed land beyond the trees. Here the many scents of a variety of bushes and ferns mingled with the perfume of the damp earth. I pushed on through low-lying branches and snaking brambles which were seeking new places to put down roots.

A pause to listen - it was another hedgehog; coming closer. And then she appeared out of the deep shadows beneath the hedge. Like all hedgehogs my night vision is my best vision and her eyes were full of curiosity as she caught sight of me.

We studied each other for what seemed like a long time. She was clearly an adult female, slightly smaller than me, and the natural earth colour a healthy hedgehog should be. She was the first to speak.

'My name is Breeze...' It was the first time I had heard a hedgehog's voice since saying goodbye to my sister Dawn so long ago.

Another hedgehog!

I replied to her introduction; 'I am Northwind.'

She chuckled, 'I can see why,' she said.

I danced around her in a circle,

I felt so full of **love**

and

joy!

And I wanted her to feel the same way too...

*   *   *

Dear Nan and Gramps,

I have got a part-time job! Well, a sort of job. I am writing a Nature Notes column for the Bugle. Nina, the new deputy editor, thought it might be something I would like to do as I go there to help out during school holidays and now that I am fifteen I am ready to try out new things.

Here is my first column which Nina said was very nice. I write them at home and email them in to the Bugle and then I pop in after school on Tuesdays and see it being put on the page. It's amazing!

I have got lots of ideas for my column. I am going to interview Lindsey of County Hedgehog Rescue and also maybe do a story on how important our local woodlands are...

We'll be coming to the city soon so I'll see you then. Lots of love, Lillie x x x x x

SPRING
ISSUE 01

Nature notes...

Many more birds are returning from Africa and Southern Europe and the garden is noisier by the day – and by the night – as the great season of life turns once again.

Compiled by Lillie Marsh

SPRING HAS SPRUNG

It is always a joy to see the buds appearing on the trees. The silver birch is covered in them, but the ash at the end of our hedge is still in winter mode with its hard black tips waiting to sprout.

New Beginnings

The snowdrops are dying back now but taking their place along the driveway are clusters of daffodils. Some have already grown heads which are yet to unfurl but the warmer days will soon encourage them to show their full beauty.

The dog fox, who we have named 'Flame' is now back on all four legs after limping for much of the winter.

He is a clever creature and has seemingly befriended our new arrival, Hero, a crossbreed rescue puppy. It's amusing and joyous to see a fox, a pup and a white hedgehog sharing the same lawn at dusk. Falstaff the cat, of course, keeps a safe distance.

At this time of year most birds are busy with the important job of nest-building. A pair of very industrious song thrushes have been singing as they work at the edge of the garden.

*   *   *

In the late evening the garden's own nocturnal air force is out and about in the shape of bats topping up on insects drawn out by the warmth of spring. I can hear their high-pitched calls but Mum and Dad cannot.

The very first time I heard a badger I thought it was a human baby crying somewhere out in the woods, so similar are the sounds. Now I'm used to it but am very nervous if they sound too near as hedgehogs are among their favourite snacks!

However, badgers are very cautious when they detect the scent of humans or dogs and so rarely venture across the lane – unlike the small group of rabbits who brave the presence of Hero and Flame in search of seeds left by our chickens.

 Look out for early bumble bees, if it is warm enough they may be out and about.

'Breeze eh? Can't say I've met her... well, obviously I haven't met her, or I'd have *ate* her!' Flame laughed a cheeky laugh and turned to me, his eyes full of mischief. 'Good old Northwind, hey - you'll be a Dad soon just like me eh?'

'I'd appreciate it if you didn't eat her you know,' I said to him.

'I promise,' he said smiling, 'Here's what I'll do - she might not think to tell me her name, so ALL hedgehogs are strictly off the menu for the whole of this season, OK?'

'Much appreciated,' I replied.

'You're welcome,' he answered, '...besides I've never seen so many rabbits as there are this year - the bouncing, big-eared b...'

A furious yapping cut him off. Black Ear had been let out of the house and had found us. The dog-cub was full of energy and excitement. Although very young I noticed he was already bigger than Flame.

'Flame... Northwind... it's meeeee!'

'Yes, we can see that,' Flame laughed as he tried to keep an eye on the young creature bouncing excitedly around us. 'I'm talking grown-up talk to Northwind at the moment; if you go and annoy the chickens for a while I'll tell you the tale later of how I led the horses through the hawthorn hedges and some human flower beds.'

'Alright' the puppy replied happily and bounded off in the direction of the chicken run, announcing his arrival all the way.

'Can't help but like him,' Flame chuckled, '...reminds me of my own cubs, wherever they are. So... Breeze eh? Will you be introducing me?'

'Not unless I bump into her again which is not really very likely, she lives on the other side of the hill behind the human nest.' I replied.

Flame studied me, head on one side, 'Not very romantic then... hedgehogs? Won't you want to see the... cubs... or whatever you call them? Prickleballs?'

'Hoglets,' I told him, 'We don't usually, fathers I mean. I never saw my father and he probably never saw his. It's just the way of things.'

Flame shrugged, 'Each to their own I suppose, still... it's nice to know they're out there somewhere.'

We fell silent for a while and listened to the busy birds shouting about how much work there was to do and how little time they had to do it. I thought about what Flame had said. Yes, it might have been nice to see my hoglets and help them by sharing my knowledge but in truth there was little I could share that would be of any help to them.

Breeze would be a far better teacher, just as my mother had once been. I thought of my sister Dawn and wondered if she too was a mother now? She would be a great one!

On an afternoon much later that summer when it was too hot to sleep in the wood shed I wandered out into the bushes that separate the human garden from the hill behind their nest.

Somewhere over that hill, Breeze would be sleeping in a proper hedgehog home with hoglets that were mine. Would she tell them about me, and how unusual their father was? I hoped so.

It would be nice to be remembered, if only for my name. I smiled and thought of Mater the hen as I imagined Breeze telling a daughter, 'You are... Bramble of Breeze and Northwind and Rivermist and Rainpuddle and Dawn...'

It was cooler in the shade of the bushes and just the right place to pull together a pile of leaves and curl up for a sleep. This is something a wild hedgehog would never do. Sleeping out in a strange place is asking for trouble but I had been caught between two worlds for so long I had lost a lot of the caution once taught to me as a hoglet.

And so, I dozed while the afternoon sun beat down and the garden shimmered in the heat.

Blue-Eye and the other hens were chattering as they enjoyed a dust bath, while somewhere overhead a pair of great black birds shouted something about following each other and going too far from home. I was warm, well-fed and content.

It was dark on waking and much cooler, but it was not the change in temperature that had stirred me. There was hot breath coming from just behind my back. I curled myself tighter into a ball and kept very, very still.

It was no fox, nor was it Black Ear the dog cub or even Zephyr. I had foolishly slept out in the open, the winds had carried my scent far and wide; a huge wave of fear washed over me.

There was no need to look behind which was just as well as I was too terrified to move. The claw that rolled me over only confirmed my dread. I had been discovered by a hunting badger.

Its claws pulled at me and forcing me to uncurl; in front of me was a face quite unlike that of a dog or a fox. Not an unkind face, but no pity either and I realised it saw me simply as another meal.

A claw tugged at me again pulling me from the cover of the hedge into the open air. In the gloom of the late evening I saw only the white stripes of its face and a twinkling within the dark stripes that gave away the position of the creature's eyes.

'My name is Northwind!' I cried as loud as I could.

It paused for a very short time as if taking in this information; then with a deep growl it resumed its attack as if the words had meant nothing. I screamed as it pinned me down with one powerful front leg and if the ground had not been soft I would have been crushed.

It paused again then as a storm broke overhead; lightning flashed, showing up the whole of the creature in all its terrible power. The rain began to pour, dripping from the branches of the hedge, soaking both of us. The creature snorted raindrops from its face and nose, shaking its striped head; black eager eyes turned back to me and a deep growl escaped as its mouth dripped in hunger...

'...Hedgehog...'

Suddenly I could not breathe or make any more sounds; the creature bared its teeth; fearsome teeth, even bigger than Flame's and I gave up the struggle, simply hoping that what was to happen would not hurt too much.

What did happen, however, took both me and the badger completely by surprise. A speeding ball of howling hair and flashing teeth crashed into the creature sending it rolling off me and on to its back. It was soon upright though and letting out a terrifying squeal, baring its own vicious teeth and turning to face its attacker.

Through my shock I now saw Flame standing between me and the badger. The hair on his back was raised, he was wild eyed and his teeth were bared; this was a Flame I had never seen before, Flame in the heat of a battle.

The thunder crashed again and lightning lit everything like a brief but dazzling sun, turning the driving rain into silver droplets. My friend screamed over his shoulder...

'Run! Run Northwind!'

But I was frozen to the spot. The badger had recovered from its shock now. It was bigger and heavier than Flame, its front legs were armed with powerful claws and it looked furious at being disturbed in such a rude and violent way.

It roared out in fury, lit by lightning, its breath throwing clouds into the silver rain, it was the most terrifying thing I had ever seen. I called back to Flame, urging him to save himself.

'Run Flame, get away!'

It was clear my friend was going to be no match for the badger. The huge black and white shape advanced slowly toward us;

'Fox...' it sneered.

But then from far behind us another sound caused everyone to stop and listen. It was the excitable and rapidly approaching barking of Black Ear. The badger suddenly looked nervous and outnumbered; it took a few steps backwards. Flame, noticing the effect the barking was having, found new heart and joined in with barks of his own.

This was too much for my attacker and with an angry cough it turned and fled through the hedge and away up the hill just as Black Ear arrived. The young dog was all for giving chase, but Flame called him back and so instead he bounced on the spot, full of the enthusiasm and energy of youth.

I was hurt, my side ached from being stood on and I walked stiffly back to the wood shed flanked by Flame and Black Ear who had clearly found a new hero.

'You're awesome, Flame, what a fox! - The bravest fox in the Great Outside!' the young dog exclaimed.

'Do you know, I probably am too,' Flame was grinning, but I had known him for many seasons and I could hear the tremble in his voice. For the second time I owed my life to him.

Seeing him prepared to fight reminded me of how hard it can be just surviving in the Great Outside and how fortunate I was to have such an easy life.

'No probably about it,' I said to Black Ear, '...he is definitely the bravest fox you will ever meet - and the best ever friend!'

* * *

20

Your Coat is Turning White

Stretching my legs while yawning is something I have always enjoyed but over the last few seasons it has begun to hurt more and more.

But after my daily sleep it was time for me to get up and see what was going on in my territory - and so a stretch was needed.

I did it slowly but still the pain in my legs spread into my back, making me close my eyes again for a second until it passed. Then, relaxing and looking around, I saw a pair of shiny black eyes peering at me from the wood pile that had been growing bigger and bigger throughout the summer.

Not a familiar face, but new mice seemed to be appearing every day, making their home somewhere safe from old Zephyr.

'Excuse me please.'

The voice was as small and nervous as the creature it came from.

'Yes?' I smiled.

'Are you... Northwind?'

'Well, yes I am,' I replied, '...and who might you be?'

The mouse took a few timid steps closer to me. 'I am Dandelion and my mother says you are so old that you were here even when my great-grandmother, Silence, was alive.'

I laughed, 'Yes, I believe that's true.'

A call from somewhere in the wood pile made Dandelion turn quickly and with a hasty, 'Goodbye - I'll come and visit you again soon,' the young mouse disappeared.

I chuckled on the way to the hole in the rear of the shed and squeezing through found myself emerging into a bright and fresh afternoon where a few early autumn leaves, were being shaken from the trees.

There was a time when sleep used to last from dawn until sunset but now that I was less active it usually ended in the middle of the afternoon.

'Off on your travels Old Hog?'

Zephyr was lazing on the stones of the path, now dried by the breeze after an overnight rain. It was the path which led to the chicken run; the damp earth meant there was a chance of a nice fat worm just outside the pen where the hens couldn't reach.

'Not as old as you,' I said passing by.

'Nine winters is not old for a cat,' he yawned and stretched out his front legs, his fearsome claws exposed. He shuddered before relaxing, '...how many for you now?'

I found I had to think about it; pausing and counting in my head before replying.

'Seven? Yes, seven - this coming one will be my eighth.'

Just thinking about the coming winter caused me to shiver. I had woken several times during the last winter. It had been a hard one, terribly cold and with lots of snow and ice and it had even felt chilly in the wood shed, despite the human heating thing.

The north wind had howled in the darkness and the brave creatures of the Great Outside had battled against fierce frosts. Then I had looked out of my nest to see Flame curled up near the heater, fast asleep on the bed Whisper had made for him.

'Seven winters... not bad for a hedgehog - or for that bony old fox either.' Zephyr smiled affectionately. Both Flame and I had been part of his life for a long, long time.

It wasn't long before I found Flame; he was curled up in Black Ear's basket under the shelter at the rear of the human nest. The basket had been put there by Whisper who now lived in another human nest far away.

She still came home in the summer and then left again when the leaves began to fall. In the winter, it was the other humans who took care of us.

Flame opened one eye as he heard me approaching. There was room in the basket for both him and Black Ear who was now several times the size of a fox and the pair could often be found curled up together.

'You're up early,' he said sleepily.

'I know,' I replied, '...I wake up and get up but then I'm tired again before I know it.'

Flame stood up, stretched and yawned, which made me yawn too, 'Change of scenery is what we need,' he decided, '...the humans have left their nest, they have taken Black Ear with them and that's a sure sign they will be away for a long time. Zephyr is asleep on the path near the chicken shed, he won't move until they come back - so how about you and I taking a slow walk up the hill to admire the view?'

And so we did. On a fresh afternoon of dancing leaves and racing clouds, my old friend and I strolled together past the chicken run where Moon, daughter of Blue-Eye, was scratching for bugs with her friends and chattering away happily.

Only a few days before Moon had told me something amazing. Apparently, the Great Outside was much greater than I had imagined. There were places very very far away that some of the birds visited where there was no such thing as winter! I envied whatever creatures lived there but was also sure they had their own dangers to face.

Up through the fence we went and across the hillside to a spot where, between two rocky slabs, stood a patch of soft grass. There was some shelter from the wind here.

I had noticed, not for the first time this season, Flame was walking stiffly and not as quickly as he used to. Was this because his bones ached the way mine now did? I would have to ask him.

From this spot it would be possible, for one with better eyes than mine, to see across the field of long grass to the wood and the river running around it. And there in the far corner of the field, the little hill where I was born such a very long time ago.

Flame sat next to me and yawned before lying down, head on his front paws, half dozing and half enjoying the view. A buzzing fly landed briefly on his nose causing him to sneeze.

'Are the white flowers out on the bush on Hedgehog Hill?' I asked.

I had always needed someone to see distant things for me but luckily Flame - as he was fond of pointing out - had the 'Best eyesight in the whole of the Great Outside!'

'Yes' said Flame, blinking into the sun.

I smiled to myself. If I had asked Flame if he could see a fly on a leaf on a tree on the far side of the woods he would have said, 'Yes,' he would never admit he was getting old.

I studied him; there was a milky haze in his eyes which puzzled me. I had never seen it there before and I realised it had been a long time since I looked - *really* looked - at my friend. When I did I saw the hair beneath his eyes and around his ears had turned white.

'Your coat is turning white,' I said.

He sniffed, 'Eh? Nonsense - you always did have terrible eyesight; and you can talk, you have been white for... well, forever.'

'I notice you are walking a bit stiffly too,' I said with concern, '...does it hurt? - It does for me.'

'Ah... yes, well - that's because I spent most of last night chasing a hare, caught him too; I decided to let him go though - he told me I was the fastest fox he had ever met!'

I turned back to the view and smiled again to myself. Flame relied on the food given to him by the humans and I could tell by the way he moved he would have little chance now of catching enough to eat.

In fact, both of us had seen more winters than a fox or a hedgehog were expected to see. All those we had known and loved seemed to be gone. Flame's parents, his brothers and sisters, even his cubs - but his grand-cubs played and hunted out there somewhere, as did my grand-hoglets I supposed.

I was surely the only one left of Mother's hoglets from that far away summer. Of course, poor Puddle had gone and there had been no news of Rain or Dawn in many seasons. Breeze too would have gone and probably my children who I had never known. Also, Mater the wise hen, Whisper the human and her old dog; all gone - although in the case of Whisper I understood she probably had a new life somewhere else as humans lived for such a long time. I wondered if she ever thought of me.

A cool breeze found us in our hiding place, a reminder of the terrible trial that always came after the falling of the leaves.

'That's a chilly wind,' I shivered.

I flattened my spines and then felt Flame's thick warm brush wrap around me.

'Better?' he asked, eyes still closed.

'Yes, thank you...' I replied. There was a silence. '...for everything,' I added.

Flame grunted something that might have been, 'My pleasure.'

It may have been the new warmth, but I was suddenly so very tired; not the usual after-hunt tired, not even a long-winter-shutdown tired; this was a heavy and irresistible tiredness.

I felt I could not hold my eyelids up and my head nodded. It was as if all the different parts of my body; my bones and skin and eyes and ears and legs and feet... even my spines, were tired.

I had never felt this way before, but I had once learned a hard lesson about the dangers of sleeping outside. Flame must have sensed this concern. He opened one eye...

'It's alright, you can sleep, I'll watch out for you.'

'But who will watch out for you?' I replied.

He smiled, and like a sudden wave of lightness, freedom and floating, came the knowledge that there really was nothing more to worry about.

So, I allowed my eyes to close and I drifted into a dream that seemed so strange and real.

Mother visited me, her voice unchanged from when I was tiny...

'Northwind, my beautiful special little hoglet; who would have thought it? You have done so well - so very, very well.'

Then Dawn appeared too...

'You are amazing Brother; all your nephews and nieces and their hoglets and grand-hoglets have heard of Northwind and his adventures. We are all so proud of you.'

'Northwind...'

The next voice was the windswept and bleak hiss of Sunn the Adder from so long ago...

'So, you managed to survive all the dangers of the Great Outside? You really have done well. This is what happens when you are polite and respectful and listen to good advice from those who know.'

Mater the hen was suddenly with me too, she clucked approvingly...

'Northwind of Rivermist and Rainpuddle and Dawn and so many others. Your name will be whispered around the Great Outside for as long as there are creatures to hear it.'

My next visitor was also an unexpected but welcome friend...

'Jack - or should I say Northwind - that's your real name, isn't it?'

It was Whisper the human and she knelt and studied me with affection (funny how I could now understand her perfectly).

'It's me, Lillie - and I will remember you for all of my long, long life. I'm sorry I had to go away but I look at your picture a lot, you were very special to me.'

Then there came a friend from long ago who once offered her life to save mine; dear little Patience whose tiny body was so full of courage and kindness...

'You have been very lucky Northwind - look how many lives you have touched and how many happy memories you have given. You have learned now that what I told you was true - do you remember...?'

'Yes - every life matters.'

'Eh?' I heard the voice of Flame, 'What did you say?'

'Every life matters,' I replied, 'I was dreaming I think.'

The sun was setting. Flame was awake and standing; I looked at him and - suddenly shocked - looked again...

He was young!

The chilly wind had dropped, and all seemed still. The colours around us seemed so... vivid, sharp and clear, colours I had never experienced before, colours I had no names for, they made it feel like the whole of the Great Outside was laughing. I stood and stretched, it didn't hurt.

'Flame? What's going on?' I asked.

He laughed a youthful laugh, so full of energy,

'Look!' he said, 'Look, across the field!'

I did - and I saw clearly, more clearly than I had ever seen. All the way to the little white flowers blooming on the bush above my birth home and while I watched a mother hedgehog emerged followed by a troupe of hoglets, one... two... three... four... five and the last two were... white! They looked up at the evening sky for the very first time and I felt their wonder.

'I don't understand... how...?'

I looked back at Flame. He was dancing on the spot, buzzing with excitement and suddenly I did understand. I felt as if I was full of butterflies, warm and energetic; the ache in my bones had gone and so I tried dancing too which made Flame laugh.

He sniffed the air and turned to me, his beautiful eyes now clear again and the colour of the setting sun. They twinkled with mischief.

'Come on,' he said, 'I'll race you to the river!'

END

*   *   *

Thank you - Diolch!

To those that have been there for and with us... Thank you.
To Rob and Julie especially. There from the off.

*   *   *

Northwind